Arthur Thomas played rugby for New Brighton. He served with the Royal Marines 45 Commando for two years of national service and joined the Northern Rhodesia Colonial Police.

Heartfelt thanks to my generous, loving and supportive wife, Sue, and my daughter, Deborah.

Arthur Thomas

Nkhwazi

Austin Macauley Publishers™
London • Cambridge • New York • Sharjah

A CIP catalogue record for this title is available from the British Library.

ISBN 9781035805914 (Paperback)
ISBN 9781035805921 (ePub e-book)

www.austinmacauley.com

First Published 2024
Austin McCauley Publishers Ltd®
1 Canada Square
Canary Wharf
London
E14 5AA

Table of Contents

Prologue

Perched on a bare branch of a giant sycamore fig, high above the water, Nkhwazi, the fish eagle, enjoyed a commanding view of his domain. Above him the sky brightened with the delicate hues of a false dawn. Others of his kind hunted this stretch of the great Kafue River but he could afford to be tolerant since the fish were plentiful and his dominance was seldom challenged. As a blaze of vivid colours burgeoned to fill the sky in the east he threw back his head and saluted the rising sun with a wild ringing call.

Then he lowered his gaze and carefully scanned the water below watching a probing finger of sunlight that pierced a gap in the dense canopy of the riverine bush and played on the surface of a calm backwater. The ray of light drew clouds of minute golden crustaceans that rose from the darkness of the depths to dance in the patch of sunlight. The shimmering movements of the daphnia attracted the attention of a shoal of slender silvery fish. The pool of crystal-clear water was soon filled with bright flashes of silver as the small tetras twisted and turned disporting themselves in a feeding frenzy.

Njuzi, the pike was almost invisible where he hovered in deep shade below a lily pad. His eyes were fixed on the feeding fish and his mouth was slightly agape, revealing serrated rows of needle-sharp teeth. Virtually motionless the predator hung in the water suspended by the gentle fanning of his pectoral fins. Then, with a sudden flick of his powerful tail, he lunged forward his vicious jaws slashing left and right. Some of the small fish succeeded in darting into cover, while others escaped the deadly jaws by leaping high in the air but not all were so lucky. Turning sharply Njuzi doubled back to snap up the numerous less fortunate individuals that had been killed or injured in his attack. Then, sated, the pike allowed his body to relax and drift, basking in the warmth of the sun, his dorsal fin barely breaking the surface of the water.

High above the sunlit arena Nkwazi chose this moment to launch himself into the air. He had watched the little drama of life and death from a ringside seat but now it was time for him to break his fast. Swooping down over the pool he lowered his feet and with perfect timing hit the pike mid-ships, his talons sinking deep into Njuzi's flanks. His claws locked and his momentum enabled him to lift the big pike bodily out of the water. Then wings flapping heavily, he carried the fish to his favoured perch where, safely ensconced and with his prey secure, he tilted his head to emit a series of triumphant calls before settling down to his meal.

Chinsali, Northern Rhodesia

Solomon Mubanga, standing in the doorway of his hut, was looking at his son Simon and thinking, *I certainly made the right choice. He is tall and slim but strong and intelligent; in fact, a son to be proud of. He looks very good in the new suit that I bought him.* It had been tough for Solomon to find the money needed to put his son through college but Simon had more than justified it. The boy had excelled at St John's both academically and as an athlete.

Simon, excited to be setting out on a huge adventure, was unaware of his father's steady regard. He stood in the middle of the track trying to catch sight of the truck that would be coming to take him to Mpika.

This was to be the first step in a journey that would eventually take him from his rural home near Chinsali to the capital city, Lusaka.

Once in Lusaka, the plan was for him to meet up with an old school friend Justin Kaluba. Justin had written to tell him that he must come to Lusaka. Apparently, things had gone well for him since he entered politics.

Justin had joined Harry Nkumbula's Northern Rhodesian African National Congress (NRANC) where he was already establishing a reputation as a front runner. Justin suggested that he could find Simon useful employment if he were to come and join him in Lusaka. In his early twenties, Simon was still very naive and had never ventured further than Kasama, the small town that was the regional centre.

He was very proud of his first name, not because it was the name he had been given at baptism but because it was a name he shared with his idol, the political activist Simon Kapwepwe. He was determined that in Lusaka he would take a new and more meaningful surname. He would make himself known to the world as Simon Ngandu. Ngandu meant crocodile in Chibemba, his home language. The crocodile was the totem of the Mukulu or 'Great Ones' of the Bemba nation.

His father had persuaded Uncle Benjamin, a cousin of his mother's, to give him a lift as far as Mpika. But when Uncle Ben did eventually come to collect him, he got into a long conversation with Solomon.

Ben was so old and shrivelled that he looked as if he was no more than a dehydrated mass of wrinkles and grizzled hair.

Simon found himself wondering how safe it could be to drive with him. However, since Uncle Ben managed to eke out a precarious living by transporting small loads of goods for the local people in his old truck, Simon assumed that he must be capable of driving to Mpika.

Since it seemed as if the old men might go on talking forever, Simon climbed up into the cab and fell asleep as he waited for them to bid each other goodbye.

Ben made heavy work of climbing into the truck, and then he explained to Simon that it took real skill to drive the vehicle.

"This type of truck is often called a 'crash-gear' Bedford. You must learn to listen very carefully until you get to hear slight changes in the sound of the engine. Now watch my feet, when the engine tone is right, I double de-clutch like this." Ben pumped his left foot in and out. "Then I crash the lever home into first gear and off we go. Now I must immediately changeup to second gear, so I have to double de-clutch again and crash the lever into the next gear."

Simon watched the performance wide-eyed and prayed it would never be necessary for him to attempt to drive this vehicle.

They were well on their way and driving slowly along the main road to Mpika when Uncle Ben told him, "You should not travel in that fine suit.

I hope you have some old shorts and a shirt to wear once you have folded your suit and put it in that suitcase."

He waved his hand out of the window and said, "Do you see that lake to our west? It is called Shiwa Ngandu, the lake of the sacred crocodiles. It is where the famous Englishman Sir Stewart Gore-Browne has built his big stone house."

"He has also built a clinic for the villagers and a very good school that awards scholarships in England to the best pupils. Gore-Browne speaks our language and he has been accepted as one of us."

"As a Bemba Simon, you should know why we Bemba place so much significance on Shiwa Ngandu.

Our people have always been superstitious about twin births and held a belief that to have twins brings bad luck.

In the old days, people would come quite openly to the lake to make a sacrifice of the unwanted twin to the sacred crocodiles. Then when the British came, they tried to put an end to the practice. However, I'm sure that there are still many villagers who come here in the dusk to offer their unwanted babies to the crocodiles."

"Uncle Ben, I'm sorry but could you please pull off to the side of the road. I think I need to have a few quiet moments. I don't know what's happening to me but I have been overcome with the strangest of feelings since we came to this place."

"That's fine, Simon; just sit back, close your eyes and accept those feelings.

I think I already know the question that is in your mind. I believe that you suddenly find you have a need to ask me if it is possible that you had a twin. The truth is that you did in deed have a twin."

"I believe that what you are sensing is the presence of the spirit of your brother. Your father has always remained a firm believer in the old ways. When your mother bore twins, he felt he had to make a choice between the babies. His decision was to keep you, so he brought your baby brother here to Shiwa Ngandu to make him an offering to the sacred crocodiles. Your mother, my cousin was a devout Christian. She did not share your father's superstitious beliefs and she could never forgive him for what he did to your twin until the day she died."

Simon eventually fell asleep in the truck.

When he opened his eyes and tried to orient himself, he found that he was in a strange hut. He was lying on his own sleeping mat and the wooden head-block was one that he had carved for himself. He looked around and saw that there was a pot of boiling water suspended over the small fire in the middle of the hut and he could smell tea. Then Uncle Ben came bustling in with a tin of tea in his hand. "Come on, Simon, it's time you got moving. You have slept like a log. I have been up for hours and I have already found a lift for you as far as Mkushi."

"But what has been happening and where are we now, Uncle Ben? Why is it that I don't remember anything after we stopped at Shiwa Ngandu?"

"We are in Mpika now, Simon. The owner of this hut is an old friend of mine.

You were already more than half asleep when we arrived, so he said we could sleep over here. I think it was just that you were overpowered by the experience that you underwent when we were at Shiwa Ngandu, yesterday.

Now, help yourself to a tin of sweet tea and we'll go and see the driver. I must tell you that he is a coloured man because I don't think you would have seen many coloureds in Chinsali. You may be surprised by his appearance since he has straight hair, grey eyes and quite a light skin. Make sure that you do not stare at him too much, that might upset him and it would not be polite. He goes by the nickname 'Tikki'."

"Tikki's grandfather was a famous muzungu (European), called 'Chirupula' Stephenson who came from the north of England and was treated as a demi-god by the Lala people. You see the Lala have a legend about three gods who shared the world between them.

While one took the east and another the west, the third one took the power to assume the shape of any animal he wished. 'Chirupula' and his close friend 'Bwana Mkubwa' Jones had a big dog baboon that went everywhere with them as their pet. In the evening, the baboon would join them in relaxing, taking a seat in a chair, drinking whiskey from a glass and smoking a pipe. When the Lala people saw this, it was enough to convince them that these were indeed the three gods of their legend.

‘Chirupula’ had also brought an N’goni wife and several children with him when he settled among the Lala. He took a Lala princess as his second wife and he had several children with her, including Tikki’s mother, Sara.”

They found ‘Tikki’ dressed in camouflage and sitting on a log next to a bright red truck. It was very much bigger and newer than Uncle Ben’s truck; in fact, it still had all its paint.

“I see you, Ben, so you finally managed to rouse this young loafer. It’s not before time, because I need to get on the road.” Tikki said, immediately climbing up into his cab.

“I see you, ‘Tikki’; this is my nephew Simon, from Chinsali. I must thank you for helping him out with a lift.”

“Up you go, Simon, and go well, both of you.”

They both wished Uncle Ben to stay well and waved as Tikki pulled the truck out onto the road. Simon soon discovered that he was travelling in luxury; he had an extremely comfortable seat and ‘Tikki’ made nothing of slipping effortlessly through the gears.

Tikki pointed to a series of great, smoothly curving domes of rock that swelled up out of the plains to the east. “I’ve heard the Europeans call those rock formations ‘whale-backs’, Simon, they are quite an impressive sight, aren’t they?”

“They certainly are, Tikki, we were taught a little about that type of rock formation at school. The magma that formed those domes was forced up from deep underground meaning that it is a plutonic rock type named after the god of the underworld Pluto.”

“The rising magma buckled but did not break all the overlying layers. It remained underground and cooled slowly to crystallise into a mixture of three different minerals, quartz, feldspar and mica."

"The composition of this rock and its speckled appearance is typical of granite. The scientific name for a granite dome that has that whale-back form is 'batholith'."

"Thanks for that information, Simon; I will be glad to have something more to tell my passengers when they ask me about those rocks."

"I can see two elephants, Tikki, they look so huge! I've never actually seen a real one before although I have seen pictures of them in books."

"Yes, Simon, they are indeed 'jumbo' and you are going to get a really good look at them because they are heading for this road. They have probably come from the river valley that runs the other side of those mountains. It is said to be teeming with game of every variety."

"When we get closer, you can tell me if the tip of the big one's left tusk is broken and his left ear is rather ragged. If it's the one I am thinking of, then I saw him receive that damage in a fight with another very powerful bull over breeding rights. They were already fighting when I came along, so I stopped to watch."

"The one I call Tembo came out on top. If he could talk about his wounds, he would probably say, you may think this is bad but you should have seen the other chap.

Anyway, that's what makes it easy for me to recognise Tembo. He is the dominant male around here. The younger bull is his askari and acts as his backup."

"They've probably been over into the valley paying a visit to the breeding herd so that Tembo could play his part in servicing the cows. His askari could only be an observer since he hasn't won breeding rights yet."

"The river that you mentioned on the other side of those mountains must be the Luangwa. Tikki, I remember learning about the Luangwa Valley National Parks at school. Luangwa North and Luangwa South are amongst the greatest national parks in our country and people come from all over the world to visit them."

"I can see that big elephant clearly now and I think he must be the one that you call Tembo.

They have stopped in the middle of the road. They are just standing there watching us closely. Do you think they mean to give us problems?"

Tikki drove up to the elephants slowly, finally cruising to a halt just a short distance from them. "You can relax, Simon, I know Tembo well. I also think he knows this truck because we often meet on this stretch of road. He has a set pattern, you will see, he shakes his head, flaps his ears and he'll probably trumpet a little. Then he will advance, coming down the road towards us in a mock charge. Basically what he is doing is showing off for the askari and at the same time letting us know who's the boss."

Sure enough, Tembo went into his little routine exactly as Tikki had described.

Then he appeared to lose interest, nudged the askari to say let's go, and the pair of them wandered off to the west.

"Tembo knows his way around," said Tikki.

"It's a veritable elephant paradise where he's heading, abundant lush green vegetation for fodder, swimming pools and mud baths galore. Who knows, those two may even go as far west as the Banguelo Swamps."

They were on the move again when Tikki asked, "What are you planning to do in Lusaka, Simon? Are you going there because you hope to find a job?"

"My school friend Justin Kaluba has asked me to come. He has joined a political party called the Northern Rhodesian African National Congress. He says that it is going well for him there and maybe I can also be usefully employed."

"I find it unusual for someone as young as you to take an interest in politics. I would have expected you to have more interest in football?"

"You're quite right, Tikki, up to now, I have mostly been interested in sport. I must tell you that when it comes to soccer, I am a keen Liverpool fan. However, since I received this invitation from Justin, I have been trying to learn more about politics and especially about the NRANC."

"I do know that the party leader is a Tonga called Harry Nkumbula. As a Tonga, I expect that he must draw a lot of his support from the southern province?"

Tikki braked sharply as a small family of warthogs erupted out of the long grass of the verge and trotted briskly across the road ahead of them.

Even the three tiny ones, closely following their mother, held their tails up ramrod straight like antennae.

The boar that brought up the rear was huge with a massive pair of tusks.

He stood proud, while his beady eyes surveyed the truck menacingly, looking for any sign of aggression. Then finally satisfied he shook himself all over and trotted off to catch up with his family.

"Sorry, Simon, before that little distraction, I think you were asking about the main areas of support for the NRANC.

You're right in thinking that they have strong support in southern province but you may be surprised to learn that they also enjoy major support on the Copperbelt especially in Mufulira."

"Being in transport, I get around the country and I hear quite a lot.

While Nkumbula himself is definitely moderate in his views, he has his hands full controlling the firebrands in his party. People will usually say, 'Oh, you must mean Simon Kapwepwe.'"

"Kapwepwe is not alone in being a militant activist. I have been at meetings where Kaunda the general secretary has been prepared to advocate violence. I don't know your friend Kaluba, Simon; however, what I do know is that politics can be a very dirty game. The word is that there is major trouble brewing in Lusaka. You must be very careful who you choose to associate with."

"I've met Harry Nkumbula, who heads the NRANC and it is my opinion that he is a good man, moderate and very sensible.

But that does not apply to many of those who cluster around him, Kaunda, the Wina brothers and that firebrand Kapwepwe, for example."

Simon, who had been brought up to show great respect to his elders, managed to keep his peace, with difficulty, when Tikki aired his views on the man who was his hero, Simon Kapwepwe.

"I see Simon Kapwepwe as a trouble maker who does nothing but instigate violence. He is liable to do more harm than good in our fight to gain a more liberal franchise."

Platres

The men of Zulu troop, 45 Royal Marines Commando were quartered in the gutted shell of the old Grand Hotel in Platres, an erstwhile mountain resort town in Cyprus.

The accommodation in the cavernous ballroom was hardly grand. Their sleeping bags lay on bare floorboards and gusts of icy wind whistled through the broken windows. The nights were frequently bitingly cold at this elevation.

A handful of marines from eighteen section squatted around a primus stove and eagerly watched a pot of water, willing it to boil so they could make a warming brew. Chilled to the bone they had spent the last four hours patrolling in the deep snow that covered the Troodos Mountains.

"It's cold enough to freeze the balls off a brass monkey," said Jack Frost.

"You can say that again," said Tom Savage. "It's so cold out there that even the galloping cruds are staying home and I didn't spot a single swinging trog tonight."

'Tiny' Small, the oversize recruit, who had just joined the section, looked at Tom wide-eyed. "Have you actually seen them sometimes then, Tom?" He asked.

"I saw a warning on the company notice-board about surviving prehistoric monsters up here in the mountains but I thought it must be a joke."

"Let me tell you about those trogs, Tiny," said Bill Sharp, "if one of them should take you down and sink his fangs in the back of your neck, you won't think it a joke. They are like giant, carnivorous, flying squirrels. Trouble is, there is no warning, you won't hear a thing until one glides up and hits you from behind."

"True," said Tom, "at least with the galloping cruds, you have plenty of warning; what with the way they grunt and snort to work themselves up before they charge."

"Aye," said Geordie Graham, "and if you manage to side step that first charge, then you'll be alright because they have to run all the way around the mountain before they can have another go at you!"

"Go on," said Tiny in amazement.

"Yes," said Jack, "the thing is when you do encounter a crud, Tiny; you must weigh it up pretty quickly. They are easy to recognise because they are massive and hairy, very much like Yaks. You only have a few moments to decide if it belongs to the clockwise or the anti-clockwise variety before it charges."

"You see, they have six legs and the three on the uphill side are shorter than those on the downhill side. Once you have managed to dodge one, it can't turn around or it will fall over and keep on rolling all the way down the mountain."

"Well, the penny has finally dropped," said Tiny, "I'm glad you've enjoyed having some fun at my expense but it's enough now. I suggest you call it a day or I'll send the whole lot of you rolling down the mountain."

"I wish you would," said Geordie, "I'm sure it must be warmer down there."

Jim Auld chimed in at this point giving them something to think about other than the icy cold;

"Well, I'm okay because I'll obviously go back to my old firm in Scotland but what plans have you guys got in mind once you're demobbed?"

Except for Tiny, the national service men were nearing the end of their mandatory two year stint.

"Well, it's a no brainer for me, I'll just go straight back into the family business," said Paul Foresight, who was heir to a major retailing empire in the north of England.

"I'm not really sure," said Tom Savage. "I do know I don't fancy going back to my civvy job. That would mean being a desk jockey in Liverpool for a few years before I could get an overseas posting."

Bill Sharp chipped in, "Well, I have no intention of being stuck in the UK. I've written to Crown Agents to apply for a post as an inspector in the Hong Kong Police. I hear that they are looking for guys of our calibre who have seen some action and had experience at leading small groups of men."

"That sounds interesting, what do you say, Geordie?" "Well, I don't know, Tom, I guess it sounds okay but this accent of mine's would probably be a handicap. Try as I may I just can't shake it and I doubt those Chinese would be able to understand me."

"True enough," said Bill. "We're your mates but when you get excited, we often battle to understand you. What about you, Pat, it's not like you to be so quiet, is it because the cold has really got to you?"

"Well, it's a grand idea so it is. In fact, I'm busy giving it serious thought. Hong Kong eh! Well, one thing's for sure it will certainly be warmer there. You didn't happen to get any idea about the pay they might be offering there, did you, Bill?"

"No, but I promise that you fellows will be the first to know all the details when I do get a reply from them."

"Okay, guys hold out you mugs, brews up," said Jim. He had used the last of their precious condensed milk, and there was just enough for each man to enjoy a hint of its creamy sweetness in his tea. As they sipped at their mugs, Jack saw Tom's hand go to the pocket of his camo jacket.

"Come on, Tom," he said, "don't tell me you're still carrying that 'Dear John' letter around! It's not as if it's anything special, we've all had them, why, Bill has had at least three that I know of. It's high time you got over it and realised that there are more important things in life than bits of skirt."

At that point, Jim closed the primus down to save fuel. Wanting to retain some semblance of warmth the friends wasted no time climbing into their sleeping bags. They needed to get some shut-eye before going out again in the small hours for another four hour patrol. There was no further discussion about a future in the Colonial Police, but the seed had been sown.

Some months had gone by during which the unit had played active roles in Cyprus and during the Suez Crisis in Egypt before they returned to their home base in Malta.

The demob of several of the national servicemen was now imminent and Bill Sharp decided to revive the subject of joining the Colonial Police.

"Well, when I get back to 'Blighty', I've already got an interview lined up at Crown Agents requesting a posting to Hong Kong," he said handing out hand-written slips of paper.

"Come on, guys, let's give it a go. That's the address for your applications and make sure you mark them for the attention of Mr E St John Shawcross."

"The 'buzz' I've heard is that you'll have plenty of chance to think about it. Apparently, the rest of the Commando will be heading back to Cyprus. But those of us who are due for demob have to undergo a final initiative test. It's going to involve getting off this island then independently making our way back to Stonehouse Barracks in Plymouth. Just as a 'heads up', I checked the map and I would suggest that you rule out swimming as an option. Sicily is a long way off and I believe we will be required to travel carrying all our basic kit."

The friends received official confirmation of this arrangement on the following day, together with the princely sum of seven pounds a head. This, they were informed, was intended to cover any expenses they may incur.

"So much for us entertaining any hopes of enjoying champagne and caviar en-route," said Jack.

"It's agreed then, after demob, those of us who decide to go with the Colonial Police idea are to meet up ASAP in Hong Kong." They shook hands on the deal.

Tom made his way to Sicily by working a passage on a small trading schooner but when the carabineeri came aboard the boat in Catania, they searched his kitbag and found his uniform. They arrested him and put him in a cell.

He was held there until later that evening when their officer returned from visiting his girlfriend. He apologised and organised a bed for him at the youth hostel.

The officer came back early in the morning to give him a lift out of town and warned him about the prevalence of bandits in the area and that he was likely to encounter some very dubious characters on the road. Tom had only walked a couple of kilometres when a very diminutive car stopped to offer him a lift. The Italian couple and their teenage daughter did not speak either English or French but Tom and the daughter eventually managed to communicate in the basic

Latin they had both learned at school. His new friends took him to Messina where he caught a ferry to Reggio.

He then went on to hitchhike the length of Italy finding that the long distance truckers were very friendly and glad to have his company.

He spent two days exploring Rome and slept in some very impressive youth hostels along the way, including one that Mussolini had once used as a palace.

Crown Agents for the Colonies

Tom had only been back at home on the Wirral Peninsular for a couple of days when he received a reply from Crown Agents regarding his application. He opened it to find that he was required to present himself for interviews at their Milbank offices on Monday morning.

It was early Sunday morning when he doubled down to the Seacombe landing stage to catch the Royal Iris, one of the black-and-white Wallasey ferry-boats that cross the Mersey to Liverpool.

Before his call-up, he had caught this ferry every working day, running quickly up the ramp to board a tram that took him to his job as a trainee manager with British-American Tobacco in Bootle.

This time, however, the tram he caught took him up Church St to the Lime Street railway station. He patted one of the famous bronze lions as he passed.

The Liverpool boys had a saying that the huge lions sitting outside the station would roar if a virgin walked past them, but Tom knew better and wasn't exactly holding his breath. On entering the station building, he bought a copy of the

Liverpool Echo then walked along the platform to board the Euston Express.

Taking a seat, he skimmed through the paper but found little of interest. An attractive Wren from HMS Drake joined him in the carriage and they chatted for a while. Then he turned his attention to the window. He found that they had left the urban sprawl behind and were crossing the beautiful rolling Cheshire countryside.

On arrival in London, he visited friends in Kensington. They had a lot of catching up to do, so he was pleased and grateful when they insisted that he spend the night.

On Monday morning, he got up very early to catch the tube. He was glad he had decided to wear a trench coat over his suit because it meant he was able to enjoy a walk along the Thames embankment despite the drizzling rain.

He studied the craft plying the river for a while then turned to watch the staff engaged in opening up Crown Agents' palatial offices. He waited, giving them a chance to settle in and have their first coffee before he crossed the road and went in to introduce himself.

At the reception desk, an elderly receptionist informed him that there were a number of forms waiting for him to complete, he found that these included several questionnaires and a variety of intelligence tests.

She handed him the forms and a pen, then directed him to a table that he could use and enquired if he would care for a cup of coffee or tea.

When Tom went back to the counter to hand in the completed forms, the receptionist placed them in a folder, stood up and told him to follow her. They went along a passage until they came to a very imposing door. "This is where you are to have your interview with the board," she told him.

"Take a seat and wait here until you are invited in." She went through the door then returned a few minutes later minus his folder. "You are lucky, it's not everyone who gets to have an interview, but you may go through now, Mr Savage."

While the huge panelled office was very impressive, Tom immediately focussed on the three elderly men who were seated behind an immense desk.

There was a chair in front of the desk but he was not invited to sit, so he simply stood easy. He could see that his folder was lying open in front of the uniformed man sitting in the centre.

However, it was the man to the right, wearing a charcoal coloured three-piece suit and a combined operations tie, who threw a box of matches onto the desk in front of him. "Talk to us about that for five minutes," he ordered. Tom felt a wave of relief. They were starting him with an easy one.

There was so much to say about what went into the materials and making of a box of matches let alone the multitude of uses for them.

He had only spoken for about two minutes when 'combined ops' said, "Yes, that's quite enough, in fact very good, indeed."

The light grey pinstripe, who was wearing a parachute regiment tie and sitting on the left said, "I see that you won a scholarship to a good grammar school, why is it that you didn't follow through with varsity?"

"There were financial considerations, sir," Tom told him.

"You seem to have focussed on sport especially rugby," said the SAS tie consulting his folder.

"I see that you played for 45 Commando RM. And you recently captained their Zulu team that won the plate in the Middle East Command Sevens." He glanced at the other members, nodded, and then said, "Very well, Savage, you can return to the reception area."

Tom reported to the receptionist who said, "Now you must see Mr Shawcross. He is down the same passage but on the right. Just sit outside his office until he is ready for you." Tom quickly found the office which had an engraved brass plate on the door announcing that the occupant was one E St John Shawcross.

After some twenty minutes just as Tom had begun to wish he had brought a book, the door opened and a young man wearing a grey pinstripe suit and a guard's tie came out, carefully closing the door behind him. Eying Tom, he wished him, "Good luck with that!"

"Well, many thanks for the good wishes," said Tom.

A few minutes later, the door opened again and this time, a short, heavily whiskered individual invited Tom to enter. The little man made Tom think of a goblin. His legs seemed to twinkle as he moved and he almost vanished when he sat down in a large chair behind the vast highly polished desk. A single slim folder was sitting on the desk and when the man picked it up and began to read he really did disappear completely behind it.

Tom sat waiting patiently looking at his name on the cover until, after some moments, the man's fuzzy head popped-up over the top of the file. "So, Savage, I see that your results are very satisfactory but apparently you have requested a posting in Hong Kong? I must inform you that there are no openings in Hong Kong at present nor are there likely to be at any time in the foreseeable future. May I therefore suggest that you give serious consideration to taking up a posting in Northern Rhodesia?"

"I know very little of that country but am I correct in believing that it would be situated in Sub-Saharan Africa, sir?" Tom asked.

St John Shawcross stood up and turned to face a vast world map that took up most of the wall behind him.

It was entitled the British Empire and in it a great deal of the world was coloured in pink. He reached up and placed a proprietary hand over the middle of Africa pronouncing, "Yes indeed, Savage, here it is in the very centre of Africa, it is a land of great rivers."

Tom tried to think of something to say that could follow on from such a dramatic statement, in the end he simply asked, "Tell me, sir, would you happen to know if the fishing is good?"

"Yes indeed, Savage, I'm quite certain you will find that the fishing is outstanding."

"That's really grand, and could you tell me, how soon would I have to go?"

"We simply require your signature on this form, since you have already met our requirements. Once the form has been submitted and accepted by the board, you will be on a flight to Central Africa within three weeks."

"Will it be in order if I hold-off on signing for now and come back later this afternoon to give you my decision?"

"Yes, that will be fine, but you must bear in mind that any delay will inevitably increase the likelihood of your being disappointed. There are a limited number of posts and I can assure you they are always taken up very quickly."

Brilliant! Tom thought, as he sat nursing a rapidly cooling mug of tea and watched raindrops trickle down the window of the little tea-shop he had discovered around the corner. Faced with a life changing fork in the road all you could come up with was 'Is the fishing good?' Even now, having played for time and when you should be honing you mind to make the best of this important decision, what are you doing!

You're sitting here pondering if it's possible that those sticky buns in the window could be as disgusting as they look?

So let's be methodical about this. What are my options?

1. Return to my desk job in Bootle.
2. Use the rest of this week to start job hunting in London.
3. Contact the St Helen's Club regarding their offer of a rugby league trial?
4. Sign up as a regular in the Royal Marines.
5. Sign up for continuous service with the Fleet Air Arm and train as a pilot.

Twenty is too young to start putting down roots and I feel ready for some more travel and adventure.

It's a pity that the Hong Kong deal isn't on the cards but it seems as if I shall have to settle for Africa! It does make sense come to think of it because the wide open spaces of Africa have always held more appeal for me than any crowded city in Asia.

His decision made; Tom paid a quick visit to Crown Agents to sign the forms.

Then he went to Foyle's hoping to find a book on the Central African Federation preferably with a comprehensive section covering Northern Rhodesia. Once there and as a life-long bird-watcher, he couldn't resist treating himself to a copy of the Birds of Central Africa. On the train and heading back up north, after a preliminary scout through his new books he spent time thinking how he could go about breaking the news to his mother and grandmother that he was off again so soon. He also had to give some thought to what he must wear, what he should pack and who he must go to see to say his farewells.

Belfast

Pat O'Brian caught a tram from Lime Street station to the Liverpool pier-head. He looked around and soon found a small cafe where he could settle down to nurse a cup of tea while he waited. He had at least two hours to kill before he could board the Irish Ferry, then it would take all of twelve hours for the crossing.

He would have plenty of time to give some thought to his future.

He had written to his uncle Paddy, a sergeant in the Royal Ulster Constabulary, about work but the response had not been very encouraging. His uncle had written to say he would find it difficult to find any sort of job in Ulster, let alone one that paid enough to enable him to support his mother and younger siblings.

Unemployment was rife in Ulster and many veterans on returning from the war had been obliged to emigrate.

He arrived home to find his uncle Paddy there sharing a cup of tea and a chat with his mother. As he came into the sitting-room, Paddy jumped up to give him a big hug. "My, my, Pat you have grown and filled out since I last saw you. Your time with the marines must have been good for you."

"Yes indeed, Uncle, they certainly made sure that we got fit."

"I don't know if I altogether approve, but I can hear that they have also got you talking more like an Englishman! Your mother has been telling me that you mentioned the Colonial Police in one of you letters. I do think that may be a good idea for you. Several of the younger chaps serving in the RUC with me have already written to Crown Agents to apply. They told me that there are a limited number of posts so if you are going to try I think you should write to them with your CV as soon as possible."

"The Colonial Police are a paramilitary force so your two years of active service with the marines should stand you in good-stead. Apparently, the Crown Agents are not recruiting for the rank and file, they specifically require officers."

"Our chaps also tell me that if you are successful with the tests and interviews you will have to undergo at Crown Agents, you will be shipped out to a British colony. Once you are there and have performed well at the training school, you will become a member of the inspectorate and receive a good salary. In any case, I certainly think you should apply."

When Paddy had said his goodbyes, Pat's mother said, "I hate this talk of you going away so soon when you have just walked through the door. However, what Uncle Paddy says is quite true, things are extremely tight here. I really appreciated the fifteen shillings we received from your national service pay especially since I realised that it was more than you could afford. But now we don't even have that and the widow's pension I receive is a pittance. To be perfectly honest, as the eldest, we desperately need you to come up with a reasonable source of income that will not only keep you but enable you to help support this family. Mike O'Donovan, two doors down, is one of the RUC lads who wrote away."

"His mother says he has already heard from Crown Agents. You should have a word with him, and perhaps he will be able to tell you a bit more about joining the colonial force."

That evening, Pat went to talk to Mike over a couple of pints of Guinness in Kelly's Cellars. The Irish pub he had dreamed of while he was away.

"I'm afraid I don't know much," Mike told him. "But I'm off to London for a grilling the day after tomorrow."

Heathrow

Sitting in an underground train on his way to Heathrow Airport, Tom Savage was thinking, okay I have seen something of Africa already, but that was mostly the northern coastline and the desert.

This will be the real Africa. For the first time, I will be venturing south of the Sahara, a land where elephant and rhino, leopard and lion roam free, the bird-life is fantastic and the fishing is great.

Who knows perhaps I may even get to spend some time on the Zambezi River and tackle one of those tiger-fish whose fighting prowess I read about last night.

The travel agents told me that a flight from London to Salisbury should take between fourteen and fifteen hours, usually with one short touch-down probably in Nairobi. That certainly doesn't jibe with the information from Crown

Agents. Tom re-read the itinerary contained in the Crown Agents letter.

Central African Airways, Flight 253, from London Heathrow-Nice-Rome (overnight flight)-Benghazi-Wadi-Halfa (stop-over and service)-Khartoum-Entebbe (stop-over)-Ndola-Lusaka. It certainly looks as if we'll be popping up and down like a yoyo!

That does beg the question, what sort of kite can we be flying in? How can it take several days with stop-overs to reach Lusaka?

Purely from my own viewpoint, I can look on that as a positive since it means that I get to see more of Africa.

When Tom arrived at Heathrow, he went straight into the terminus and looked around for any sign that might relate to Central African Airways.

His search was unsuccessful but he did find a manned enquiries desk. When he asked about his flight, the ground hostess on duty apologised. "I'm sorry sir, I'm afraid I am not familiar with CAA. Please wait for a moment or two while I search through the data sheets. Ah! Yes, here we are." She pointed down the long row of airline counters, "You must proceed all the way down this concourse and you will find them at the very end."

Tom arrived at the CAA counter to discover that it was closed and another passenger was standing around. The man had a military bearing and when he turned Tom saw and recognised the white daggers on his green tie. "Hello there, I see you served with 40 Commando. I'm Tom Savage and I was with 45."

"Hi, Tom, I'm Rob Auld, I'm heading for the Northern Rhodesia Police training school at Lilayi, near Lusaka, what about you?"

"That goes for me too, Rob, we'll be sure to get off to a good start with a couple of marines in the squad. It looks as if we could be a while and there's no seating here, so I suggest we go and commandeer a couple of loose chairs from the main concourse."

When they had brought the chairs and parked them near the vacant CAA counter, Tom asked, "Were you based in Paphos, Rob?"

"Yes and my guess would be that you were either in Platres or Troodos?"

"That's true enough, in fact, I spent some time in both," said Tom.

"In that case, you may be able to tell me if there any truth in a weird tale I heard. It seems that Zulu Troop managed to kill off a priceless donkey when they were guarding the signal station up on Mount Olympus?"

"Well, Rob, that is a bit close to the bone, but since we have time to kill and we're both marines, I'll tell you that I played a part in that fiasco. You see a new recruit, recently out from UK, came to join my section when we were up on the mountain."

"Of course, we fed him the usual stories. We told him he must always be on his guard and aware of the danger of encountering one of the prehistoric monsters that still lurked in the mountains."

"Even our CO viewed these tales in a positive light. He had a national serviceman, who was a cartoonist by profession; draw up an identification chart that also gave advice on how to behave when encountering one of them. Copies of the chart were run off and placed on the HQ and troop notice boards."

"In addition to being a bit of fun, these stories served a purpose since they helped to keep the new boys alert, especially at night when they were on guard duty up there among the tall trees. From time to time, we had to take our turn guarding the signals station that sat right on top of Mount Olympus. It was really cold up there and night temperatures could be as low as minus 15 degrees."

"On the night in question, my half-section had the midnight to 4.00am watch. I posted the new guy, who we'd nicknamed 'Tiny', because he was very large and his surname was Small, at the main gate simply because he hadn't learned to ski yet. I reminded him that he must be sure to challenge any intruders in all three languages; English, Greek and Turkish **halt, stammata, dur** at least three times before opening fire."

"Then my 'oppo' Geordie and I set off to carry out a patrol around the camp perimeter, with me going clockwise and Geordie anti-clockwise. We met high up at the back of the camp, there were no problems to report so we were feeling relaxed. We had just begun to swap some typical 'bullshit' when, clear as a bell; we heard Tiny call out the challenge, 'Halt. Stammata, Dur,' his voice kept getting higher and by the third repeat he was running the words together. Then, quick as a flash, he followed up with a short burst of fire from the Bren-gun. We went flat out, straight through the middle of the camp, to the main gate. When we got there, we found Tiny crouched behind the sandbags shouting, 'It's the first time I've shot anything. It was a "crud", I'm sure it was a "galloping crud"! I challenged it three times, Tom, but it just kept coming.'"

"We could hear strange noises coming from a dark heap lying out on the snow. When we went out to it, we found an ancient donkey in the process of breathing its last. An old donkey like that usually sells for about five shillings in Cyprus for use as dog food."

"However, when the locals got to hear that it had been shot by a Brit, that donkey suddenly became the prize stud of the region. The headman swore that it had sired all their best donkeys and it was worth a fortune. In order to pacify them, the CO eventually had to pay the village elders ten pounds as compensation. The locals rejoiced and held parties that went on for days afterwards."

Heathrow

"To change the subject, Tom, have you managed to pick up anything worthwhile either in newspapers or magazine articles that might help us to get a handle on the current situation in Central Africa?"

"No, and I must confess, Rob, that I haven't even looked. However, I did go into Foyles and I bought quite a comprehensive book."

Rob jumped in. "Tom, its current information that we need and you won't find that in any book. We're going in there as policemen, not academics! Firstly we will need to have a good grasp of the 'status quo' and of the forces in play there. Then we can begin to develop a feel for the direction in which things are moving. I assure you this is not going to be a routine, 'bobby on the beat' type of job. I have already read one of the papers I bought so I will let you have it. It won't help you sleep at night but you're certain to find it interesting. You should read the editorial first it may give you something of an overall insight into the situation."

"Northern Rhodesia is much larger than Southern Rhodesia and Nyasaland combined and it is infinitely richer. The Africans there have been strongly opposed to the formation of a Central African Federation with the power based in the south all along."

"It was created entirely without their consent despite the fact that they constitute the vast majority of the population. They believe that the federal government intends to deprive them of their land and cattle since that has always been their form of wealth. They are also aware that the constantly cash-strapped Salisbury administration is already using the financial reserves of the north to upgrade their own infrastructure."

"Those funds were originally intended to build the road systems so urgently needed to open up the vast and largely inaccessible north. Of course, this aspect rings true and it is almost certainly the reason that the Southern Premier, Sir Godfrey Huggins pushed so hard for the formation of a Central African Federation. The British were positive about the federation provided it included the financially dependent state of Nyasaland."

"Thanks for the brief, Rob; I would like to take you up on your offer of that paper, as you say we certainly need to be in touch with the current situation in Northern Rhodesia."

"Heads up, Tom, I see we have incoming and I would say it looks very much like a 'coat-hanger'."

A quick glance sufficed for Tom to recognise that marching towards them was the same young man he had encountered at Crown Agents. "Well spotted, Rob, he's a guardsman alright and my guess is that he's soon going to be one of us."

"Tom Savage!" The voice was familiar and Tom spun around to find 'Jack' Frost descending on him from starboard, a delighted grin plastered all over his face. "This is fantastic, Tom, though it does seem that you are also a bit off course for Hong Kong."

"Very true, but it's really great to see you here, Jack, this is Rob Auld of 40 commando and Rob, this is Jack Frost of 45."

He turned back to the guardsman who had just come up to join them.

"You and I met at Crown Agents but I never did get your name?"

Tom held out his hand, "I'm Tom Savage and this is Jack Frost we were both with 45 Commando, Rob Auld here was with 40."

"Many thanks, Tom, and hello chaps; I'm Ivor Jones, lately of the Welsh Guards."

Jack said, "I must tell you, Tom; I've heard from a couple of our guys. Both Geordie and Pat wrote to Crown Agents applying for posts in the Colonial Police. Pat was called in for interviews and was successful, but they turned down Geordie's application. The fact is I was hoping Pat would be here this evening."

Tom said, "There is time and he may still join us because the counter hasn't even opened yet."

The CAA counter still remained obstinately closed when an attractive young lady arrived. Rob promptly offered her his chair, introduced the group to her and asked for her name. "I'm Jean Milner," she told them, "and I'm flying to Southern Rhodesia to meet up with my fiancé."

By now, a number of passengers had arrived and they all turned towards the counter when the shutter finally rolled up to reveal two CAA staff members in smart navy blue uniforms. It was immediately apparent that they were not ground staff.

The rings on the man's sleeve indicated that he was a captain and the winged emblem on the lady's jacket probably meant that she was an air-hostess.

"Good evening, lady and gentlemen, I am your pilot Mike Wilmot, and your hostess here is Joan Grey, we will be your crew for this flight together with my co-pilot Joe Newcombe who is to join us shortly. Please make sure you have your tickets, passports, vaccination certificates and any visas where necessary at readiness for Miss Grey who will be handling the paperwork. We will be flying in a Vickers Viking aircraft."

"For the technically minded, the Viking is a twin-engine propeller driven aircraft with a wingspan of approximately 90 feet and a fuselage that is 63 feet in length. It has a maximum carrying capacity of twenty-four passengers and a crew of four."

"Fully loaded, it has a ceiling of 10,000 feet and it cruises at a speed of 210 miles per hour. Flying at that altitude and speed, you will have the opportunity to truly appreciate the beauty and variety of the African continent. I think we must be almost up to complement now so we will start the boarding procedures." The co-pilot Joe had arrived as the pilot was giving his talk and he immediately set to work checking in the passengers' baggage.

Tom and Jack held back and let the other passengers go ahead still hoping for some sign of Pat. "I can see we are still shy of one passenger," said Joan, "and the way the pair of you keep looking down the concourse, I presume he's one of yours."

"Just give him one more minute please, Miss, I can see him running towards us."

"Very well, but you two must give me your documents in the meantime."

She opened the first passport saying, "I see this is a British passport but why was it issued in Malta?"

"That's right," said Tom, "I was serving with the Royal Marines and renewed my passport in Valetta."

She read, "Thomas Savage, five foot eleven inches, hazel green eyes and dark brown hair."

She noted the details and the work permit number then picked up the second passport and read, "Issued in London, Jack Frost, five foot ten inches, brown eyes, and brown hair." She noted those details and the number of Jack's work permit then handed back their documents.

Meantime, Pat had arrived at the counter totally out of breath. He began to explain about bad connections but the hostess merely said, "That's all very well, sir, but please give me your documents. You can save your story until we're in the plane."

The four marines joined the line of passengers trooping out onto the tarmac. Flight CAA 253 was standing on the apron waiting for the passengers to embark.

It looked like a toy in comparison with the airliners parked next to it. There were no ground staff, and the air-hostess shepherded the passengers aboard while the pilot and co-pilot, acted as baggage handlers, loading the luggage into the hold of the plane.

CAA Flight 253

Once the luggage was aboard, the passengers went up a short ramp to enter the plane through a door at the tail end. The plane was smart in its silver and navy blue livery but it looked tiny when Tom compared it to the Lockheed Super Constellation that was next in line or the de Haviland Comet that was warming up at the end of the runway. *Those airliners make our Viking appear as diminutive as a toy,* Tom thought.

Well what do you know? It was a close run thing and I almost gave up at times, thought Pat as he entered the cabin. A bus, a boat and two trains, all of them difficult connections, I feel as if I ran most of the way, but here I am at last.

He looked around as he waited for the passengers ahead of him to take seats. A narrow passage ran the length of the cabin that was equipped with single seats to port and double seats to starboard. There seemed to an obstruction in the passage up front that the passengers going forward had to negotiate. He thought, *In any case what's wrong with these three seats, they are in line, vacant and right here.*

Of course, our ride may be a bit bumpier because they are virtually at the tail but that's not going to bother us.

Also there are advantages to be gained by sitting here, not only will we be closer to the 'head' but it's handier for service. It also means I'll be well placed to chat to our hostess. True, she gave us a bit of a 'starchy' reception but I believe that can be put down to the stress of getting us all into the plane. One thing is for sure she's very easy on the eye.

Unaware of being studied, Joan Grey, as the last to climb on board, was busy carefully closing and locking the door behind her.

The plane began to taxi and after a few preliminary clicks the pilot came on the intercom. "Good evening and welcome aboard flight CAA 253, ladies and gentlemen. We have clearance and we are moving onto the runway. Once we have taken-off and attained our cruising speed, you will be given a biscuit and the choice of tea, coffee or a beer while we are en-route to Nice. Thank you for your attention and enjoy the flight."

When Joan came to see what they would like to drink, the marines ordered beers. Pat asked, "Can you tell me why this plane has that step that cuts across the aisle? I should think it must make it very difficult for you when you are serving drinks?"

"It's Pat O'Brian, isn't it?"

"Well, Pat, as you say, it is tough having to go backwards and forwards over that main spar for hours on end, especially when I'm carrying trays of drinks. I deal with it by seeing this plane as a tribute to the wonderful Vickers Wellington bombers and their crews who made such a contribution towards defeating Germany in WWII. The Wellingtons drew a lot of their strength and ability to take flak from the fact that the central wing spar passed right through the body of the plane. Vickers retained that strong wing structure and many other Wellington features when they designed this plane."

Tom had taken a seat on the port side and he was looking out at the navigation lights of shipping in the channel.

He thought, *I wouldn't mind betting it took Pat the best part of two days to get to Heathrow from his little patch of peat in the bog.*

Also he probably didn't have a chance to organise anything more than a quick cup of coffee. Tom dug about in his overnight bag and found a Mars bar. "Here you go, Pat, don't worry because I've got two and I'm betting that skimpy little biscuit you just had didn't touch sides."

The touch-down at Nice was so short; it was literally a case of touch and go. They soon climbed back to their cruising altitude with Joan busily handing out small packs of the typical tasteless airline food.

There was an equally brief touch-down in Rome. Then when they regained their cruising altitude, Joan tried to tempt them with a glass of the wine that was on offer. But the marines were unanimous in deciding to settle for another round of beer.

Pat was so tired; he fell asleep as soon as he had finished his beer. Jack was not far behind; he could always sleep, at the drop of a hat regardless of where ever he was. Tom could tell from his breathing that Rob was also fast asleep so his offer of a newspaper would have to wait. He pulled out his book and began to read about the population of Northern Rhodesia. He soon saw that there were too many different tribes and languages to grasp it all at a single reading.

He decided it would be best taken it in small doses, working clockwise and beginning with the Northern Province. Even in the Northern Province there were evidently numerous different tribes, the most important being the

Bemba group and Chibemba was the main language in that region. The Bemba group acknowledged a Paramount Chief with the title of Chitimukulu. It was tradition that the Paramount must originate from a select Bemba sub-group, who belonged to the crocodile totem. Named the Mukulu (great ones), they were the Bemba equivalent of a royal family. The Bemba people originated from West Africa and their Paramount Chief Chitimukulu owed fealty to the great Mwata Yamvwa who ruled the huge Lunda-Lubwa kingdom.

They were a warrior people and as they migrated south and east, they extended their empire by raiding and fighting. The many tribes they subdued were forced to pay tribute to them. In broad terms, from the viewpoint of the colonial administrators, they had now become the Bemba, Bisa, Lala, Lamba, Lima, Lunda, Luvale Group that shared many similarities in their languages and their culture.

Clashes with both the N'goni, a warrior people who had migrated from the south and the forces of the British South Africa Company, eventually brought the expansion of the Bemba Empire to a halt.

Wow, thought Tom, *if I am to deal with all of those unfamiliar names that is certainly enough for one session.*

Their touch-down in Rome was brief. Before they took off again, Joan went up to the front of the cabin and informed the passengers that, since they were about to fly across the Mediterranean, she must demonstrate the use of the life jackets. After a brief demonstration she told them, "In the morning, we will disembark in Benghazi, where you will have the opportunity to stretch your legs and have some breakfast. For now, all the lights are about to be switched off and it is time for you to catch up on some sleep."

The false dawn was lighting the sky and they were approaching the African coast when Pat surfaced from a deep sleep. He glanced over and saw that Tom was already reading his book. He was not surprised to see that Jack was still out for the count.

Seeing he was awake, Joan asked, "I'm making a coffee for Tom would you care for one?"

"That's definitely a yes and thank you," said Pat.

Rob Auld was also awake and turned in his seat to say, "Would you be as kind as to include me in that request, Joan?"

"Fine, Rob," said Joan, "but this is definitely the last order, we are going to begin our descent any time now."

Mike put the plane down on the Benghazi strip as light as a feather and announced over the intercom, "Good morning. ladies and gentlemen and welcome to Benghazi."

When the marines first put their feet on Terra Firma after fourteen hour in the plane, they found that their legs felt like over-cooked spaghetti. The guardsman had made his way rather shakily down the ramp so Jack took his arm and said, "Come on then, Ivor, you can join us for a march across the tarmac and a fierce engagement with a nice plate of bacon and egg. Come to think of it, I remember when we spent some time in Libya on desert warfare exercises."

"We got into town to find that they don't serve bacon because they are Muslim. Never mind, I'm so hungry I could murder a plate of macon, beef sausage and eggs."

Tom and Pat were relishing the crisp early morning air as they stepped out across the landing strip together. "Well, Pat, here we are, setting foot on Africa again. I can't help but wonder where Bill Sharp might be now? After all, it was his talk of the Colonial Police and Hong Kong that set the ball rolling. However, events beyond our control have brought us here to play out our part on an entirely different field."

Mkushi

My home is this side of Mkushi, Simon. I hope you will come with me to meet my family and have a meal with us. Then I will take you to the truck stop where you may be lucky enough to get a lift all the way to Lusaka. However, even if you only get as far as Kapiri Mposhi, that little town is on the main road between the Copperbelt and Lusaka. From there, you shouldn't have a problem finding transport to take you to your journey's end.

Mkushi was one of the main truck stops on the Great North Road. Simon found some shade and stood watching the activity. He had hoped that Tikki might stay and try to organise a lift for him, possibly with someone he knew.

Instead Tikki had just wished him well as he dropped him off in the parking area. It took him a while to get used to the fact that for the first time in his life he had no one to mentor him. He had thought that it would be exciting but now that it was a reality he found it very scary.

He had been watching the truckers closely and found that without exception they were big, rough and preoccupied. He could not imagine himself approaching any one of them to ask for a lift. He realized that he had taken the lifts with Uncle Ben and Tikki for granted. Now, he had to organise a lift for himself and it had suddenly become a very big thing.

He thought, *There may be a bus.* They had passed a bus when he was riding with Tikki. He remembered that it had written on the side, Long Distance Bus, Mbeya—Lusaka so that was international. He wondered where he could enquire about local buses even if it meant that he would have to spend some of his precious money.

Then an old truck filled with labourers pulled in close to him and two of them jumped off the back. It was clear from the banter of those still on the truck that they had stopped to buy buns and coke from the little store.

They were quite a mixture of tribes Lala, Bisa and Senga and Simon felt sufficiently encouraged by the fact that they were all speaking Chibemba to ask where they were going? When their foreman told him that they were going to Kapiri Mposhi he asked if he could join them in the back of the truck. Bring another coke and you'll be welcome he was told. Simon ran to get a large coke and climbed into the back of the truck.

Once they got underway the foreman Enoch launched into the basic questions that are asked in Africa when meeting a stranger on the road. I see you, where have you come from and why are you leaving there, where are you going and why are you going there? Having answered these questions he found that he was quite readily accepted and the men reverted to a discussion that had obviously been underway before they stopped at Mkushi.

Several of them had been present at a rally where they had been addressed by Kaunda. One or two of them expressed an opinion that they didn't consider Kaunda to be a true Bemba since his parents were from Nyasaland.

They had only moved to the mission at Lubwa near Chinsali when the Presbyterian minister they had worked with, was posted there. Be that as it may this was Simon's patch and he knew that Kaunda, as their youngest child, was born and grew up there. He was fluent in Chibemba and had attended the mission school at Lubwa near Chinsali where his parents taught.

"Regardless of that," said Enoch, "he has promised us Kwacha (freedom) when the ANC come into power."

"That's all very well," said a grizzled elderly man, "but what does he mean by freedom?" That brought a storm of response from the labourers. They all had their own ideas of what they understood to be freedom. "I'll never have to work again said one and that brought a chorus of agreement, 'None of us will ever need to work again.' 'I'll just go into a bank, write on a piece of paper like the whites do and they will give me all the money I want,' said another."

"'That won't matter,' said a third, 'because everything will be free.' 'It means that the government will give me a big house built of bricks and a car,' said a fourth."

Simon saw that these were very simple people. He knew that you had to sow before you could reap. You had to have put money in the bank before you could draw and you could only draw against what you had in there. He also knew that this was not a time to comment. He must rather sit and wait, listen and learn how the rural majority thought. The debate was lively, the miles passed quickly and soon they reached Kapiri Mposhi. They all climbed out and Simon thanked Enoch profusely. He then wished all of them very well as they went their various ways.

Kapiri Mposhi

Simon had read about trains and seen pictures but he was fascinated to be in the presence of his very first steam train. It stood in a siding next to the road with steam billowing around its engine.

"Yes it will be going to Lusaka." "He found Enoch was standing next to him holding a brown paper bag with something from the bottle store that he had disappeared into a minute or two ago. 'It's a goods train, so they are slow and they don't take passengers. If you were to hide in one of the trucks you may get a free ride but if they catch you then you will be in trouble.' I must admit I've done it a couple of times myself and managed to avoid being caught. The secret is to choose one of the middle trucks as far away from the guard or the driver as possible then wait to jump in when the train is moving. At the other end don't wait for the train to stop but jump off while it is still doing a fair speed. I saw that the fireman is busy building up the fire and they already have quite a head of steam so this one should be leaving soon.

I must be on my way now so go well Simon whatever you decide.'

Thank you so much Enoch and stay well."

As Simon walked north along the road he was thinking deeply. He checked the guard's van as he passed it.

When he had walked for quite some distance, he crossed the track and started walking back to the train on the opposite side.

He thought, *What an adventure, imagine me pulling into Lusaka riding on a steam train. I really think I might do it.* I saw that the trucks have sliding doors so I will test them as I walk past on this side. Should I find one that opens I will take it as a sign. A thought flashed through his mind. *It so unlike me to contemplate taking such a risk could it be that this is my twin's thinking?* He was just two cars from the engine when a door that he tried slid open quite easily. The car was empty except for a big heap of straw at one end. He thought, *I could bury myself deep in that straw and be well hidden.* I must leave this door open just enough for me to climb in once the train is moving. Simon strolled off into the bush as if he were going to answer a call of nature and he was sitting on a dead log under an acacia tree when the driver gave two blasts on his steam whistle as a warning that the train was about to move. He ran back through the scrub and arrived at his chosen door just as the train was beginning to pick-up speed.

Simon threw his case into the car then launched himself at the opening. It was quite high but he managed to get his elbows on the floor of the car then wriggled his body forward. Once he was in, he hid his pack deep in the straw, and then he went to sit in the doorway watching the bush slip by.

He thought if you are living an adventure this must be the ideal way to go to Lusaka.

It seemed as if it was only a few moments ago that he had come to stretch-out on the straw for a while.

He realised that he must have fallen asleep and now the train had come to a standstill. Surely this couldn't be Lusaka already. He was about to go to the door to check when he heard someone outside. There were at least two of them and they were talking very quietly in ChiBemba. A deep voice said "this door is open, come on Jackal I will boost you." Simon slithered to the back of the car and hid himself by burrowing into the straw.

"A different, much higher voice said 'it's empty in here, there's just some straw, so come on up.'" Peering through the stalks of straw Simon watched as a huge silhouette appeared in the doorway effectively blocking out the night sky.

The deep voice said 'I'm starving, here's the back pack Jackal, scratch around and see if we've got anything left to eat.' It was obvious that ChiBemba was their home language but more than that Simon felt that there was something vaguely familiar about the big man. Suddenly Simon said 'Lubwa Mission!' He was so excited he didn't realise that he had spoken out loud. The men spun around alarmed 'who's there, demanded Jackal,' peering into the darkness at the end of the car. Simon emerged from his hideout in the straw. "Don't worry Petros, it's only me Simon, you must remember me, you and I were good friends at the Lubwa Mission School."

The train was getting underway again and Petros opened the door wider to let in more light. He said "come over here where I can see you better." He took Simon by the shoulders and turned him towards the doorway. "By all that's holy it really is you Simon." He took Simon's hand in his great paw and pumped it up and down enthusiastically. "This is wonderful, Jackal I want you to meet a good friend of mine, Simon Mubanga, from Chinsali." They exchanged the complex African handshake. "But Simon, this is very strange, what are you doing in Broken Hill and hiding in a goods train? The last I heard of you was that you were working as a legal clerk in Chinsali."

"I left that job because I could see it was a dead end with no future for me Petros.

Then I received a letter from Justin Kaluba, you'll remember him, he was a year or two ahead of us at school. He said that he is in Lusaka and doing well in politics. He has invited me to come to the city and work with him."

“But this is incredible Simon; Justin is the leader of our action group in the NRANC. Jackal and I are just returning from a recruiting mission in Broken Hill. You see, we have no shortage of members but most of them are either unwilling or too afraid to play an active role in our struggle. We need to enlist many more people who will not only take up our cause but be prepared to take action and even to employ violence should that be necessary.”

He checked his watch, “it’s after midnight now and we should try to get some sleep. We will take you to meet with Justin when we get into Lusaka in the morning.”

Simon lay awake long after the others had fallen asleep. It was his troubled thoughts and not Petros’s thunderous snores that prevented him from sleeping. He had headed for Lusaka in the expectation that Justin was going to offer him a role as his aide-de-camp or personal secretary. However from Petros’s simple declaration it would seem that they were engaged as active freedom-fighters. The fact that they said Kaluba was their leader had forced him to see Justin in a very different light.

Simon was not violent by nature. He had often imagined himself returning home to a hero’s welcome after successfully bringing freedom to his people. However he had never envisioned that he may be required to play an active role in any conflict that might be involved in bringing this about. At the mission school, he had quickly attached himself to Petros who had always enjoyed a scrap and been only too happy to fight his battles for him. His thoughts then turned to the weird character of Jackal. It seemed strange but he had never really paid much attention to this odd person at school. Then he recalled that Jackal had always been so completely attached to Petros that he had come across as being as much a part of the huge man as his shadow.

Benghazi

"Knowing Bill Sharp as we do, Tom, there's no denying that he would have stopped at nothing to realise his plan of joining the Hong Kong Police. Remember, he had quite a head start on us in his dealings with the Crown Agents, so my guess is that he may have been successful in his application and managed to gain a post in Hong Kong before they shut up shop."

"If that's the case, Pat, I say he was on the ball and good for him. Who knows once we really become part of the Colonial force, we may even hear news of him. Meanwhile, let's go find this restaurant and order some of that macon and egg."

They joined Jack and Rob who had organised a table then looked up to find Ivor advancing on them with two additional 'coat-hangers' in tow. "It looks as if we'll need to do some furniture moving," said Tom.

"Let's close ranks with that other table and re-shuffle the chairs."

Ivor's group arrived in time to lend a hand with the chairs then he introduced Sam Black and Mac Duffy lately of the Grenadiers. They settled down to get to know one another over coffee while they waited for breakfast. "I know you've been telling me it's not bacon they are frying up back there," said Mac, "but if you ask me, to a hungry man, it still smells pretty good."

"Back on Flight 253 and it sounds as if today is going to be a really grand day," said Pat, who had spent some time at the rear of the cabin chatting to the hostess.

"We'll be landing at Wadi Halfa before long and it seems we're going to be there for a while because the plane has to undergo a service. That will mean staying overnight so we'll have a chance to look around, stretch our legs, try some of the local food and even get to sleep in a bed."

"I wouldn't bank on that, Pat; you may have to settle for a bunk."

Joan came over on the intercom to announce, "Ladies and gentlemen, we will shortly be landing in Wadi Halfa. You will have some free time this afternoon with the choice of a number of interesting options as to how you should spend it. You may wish to explore the Souk a market where the merchants display a wide range of hand crafted goods and curios."

"For those who are really serious about stretching their legs, my colleague Joe has volunteered to lead a climb to the summit of the hill that dominates the town and commands fine views. Finally, those with an interest in antiquities may wish to join me on a cruise and the exploration of an ancient ruined temple further along the Nile."

"As to the practicalities, I am afraid that the accommodation in the hotel is very limited. The overflow from the hotel is therefore to be housed in an old houseboat that is anchored on the Nile. Fortunately, we have a group of young men with us who have undergone the hardships of military training."

"They will probably find the accommodation on a Nile houseboat quite luxurious. The evening meal, if taken at the hotel, is courtesy of CAA, but for those choosing to experiment with the delights to be found at the restaurants in the Kasbah, they must pay their own way. Now would you please fasten your seatbelts as we are about to land in Wadi Halfa."

Joan's cruise was a full house with all the NRP recruits opting for it. The pleasant afternoon on the river was enlivened with lots of banter as the young men vied with each other to hold Joan's attention.

The small dusty temple ruin was quickly dealt with.

The decision to return to Wadi for a shower then meet for beers on the hotel veranda met with unanimous approval.

There were fourteen of them, so they quickly moved furniture to make up a long table. Introductions were made and it transpired that they had all completed their national service either in the guards or the marines with the solitary exception of Doug Egleton who had served with the RAF Regiment.

Ivor waited until everyone was settled and had a beer before speaking about the training they were about to undertake.

"I'm already bilingual in English and Welsh plus I have a fair knowledge of French but I still anticipate that the African language course may be something of a challenge. The notes we received state that we are to be given a limited amount of time to master Chinyanja, the second language of Northern Rhodesia. They stipulate that in order to qualify, we must be able to read, write and speak that language to a satisfactory degree within our first year. I must say that to attain that standard in such a short time sounds like quite a tall order."

Jack Frost said, “As far as I’m concerned, it’s equitation that bothers me most. I’ve always been scared of horses and now it seems we have to look on them as a mode of transport!”

“I would say that it’s the drill that is going to be interesting,” said Mac.

“That will definitely shake up the marines amongst us. They don’t even lift their knees when they come to attention; they just click their heels together.”

“Just try slamming your feet down on the deck of a warship as you guards do and you won’t be very popular,” said Pat.

“I’ve also had another look at our Lilayi program, Police Procedures, Police and Civil Service Law, Chinyanja, Native Customs, etc., etc. Well, one thing we can say is that it certainly seems to be a well-rounded course,” said Tom. “Personally, I’m looking forward to the advanced driving. Given our backgrounds, I’m sure we must all feel confident that we don’t have a great deal to learn about using small arms effectively.”

No one had slept well on the plane, so when they had eaten a hotel meal and had a final beer, they made their way down to the boat. The bunks were comfortable and Tom fell asleep almost immediately but he was woken a couple of times during the night by large, quarrelsome rats. Then a large feral cat put in an appearance and that soon put an end to the rats’ nonsense.

Lusaka Station

“Wakeup, Simon! We have to get moving. The railway police mustn’t see us when we jump off the train or they will arrest us and we'll be in big trouble. Also you need to pull yourself together before we have our meeting with Kaluba." Simon looked around him feeling bemused, so this was a city, he had never seen anything like it. The buildings were so numerous and tall, many of them as much as several storeys high.

"Come along now, Simon, we must begin by going to our flat. We have ablutions there where you can get cleaned up and changed.

It is very convenient that the offices of the NRANC are on the ground floor of our building."

The lift was not working so once Simon had changed; they made their way back down the stairs. A rough square of cardboard that stated ZANC was taped on the front door of the office.

When they entered, they found Kaluba seated at his desk looking very well fed and professional in a charcoal suit, grey dress shirt and a deep red tie. He stood to greet Simon.

"It is good to see you after so long, Simon; I trust your parents are well? It is fortunate that you have arrived at this time since I already have an important target for you. Transport has been arranged to take you and your team to the Copperbelt this afternoon. You should know that the timing of this project is crucial."

"You must undertake the necessary preparations for it as a matter of urgency. I have ensured that you will have excellent support. To begin with, I am giving you these two experienced agents, Petros and Jackal. They will be the nucleus of your team. Furthermore our numerous supporters in Mikomfwa have been notified that they must be ready to accommodate you. They have been instructed to procure the track-laying tools you will need for your task and to be of assistance to you wherever necessary. Now come over here with me." Kaluba walked over to a huge map that completely took up one wall of his office.

"Rhodesian Railways run one southbound main-line passenger train a day that departs every evening from Ndola station. At the end of school holidays, that train will be filled to capacity. You must take a very good look at this map and memorise the target area."

"You will see that there is a high embankment just here, where the main-line of rail from the Copperbelt crosses a high bridge over the Kafulafuta River. A derailment at that point will plunge the train, packed with hundreds of privileged children returning to schools in Rhodesia and South Africa, into a crocodile infested river."

"Of course, the media is sure to seize on a huge tragedy of that nature and they will make a meal of it. The news headlines will create an international uproar that is certain to bring our cause to the attention of the whole world. Now, let us consider the logistics that this will require. You should be aware that a project of this nature involves a great deal of research and planning if it is to be successful."

"The map clearly shows that the Kafulafuta flood plain is very extensive at that point. That means it won't be possible for you to make use of a vehicle to gain direct access to the proposed site. The final approach must therefore be made on foot. The driver, Amos, will take you to the end of the nearest track, just here where it reaches the edge of the flood plain. That will be your rendezvous. He will remain in that position until first light. If you still haven't returned by that time, he will resort to plan B, and go back to Ndola, where he will wait for me to make contact."

"The track-laying equipment is relatively heavy and your team will be obliged to carry it for quite some distance. You will have to help carry some of the smaller tools and to make sure that you allow ample time for rest periods. There are numerous buffalo and hippo in that area and they will have made game trails through the elephant grass. Since all of their trails will eventually lead to the river you should just choose one to follow. Take this compass; it will help you keep on course. Make sure that you do not waste time when you arrive at the site. Act quickly and efficiently to remove the fish-plates from the off-side rail, take out the coach-screws and lever the rail out of line."

"Once the track has been sufficiently displaced, you should dump the tools in the swamp. Then you must immediately make your way back to meet up with Amos. He will keep the vehicle waiting for you at the drop-off point until first light."

"If for any reason you should fail to meet up with the vehicle in time, then you must make your way to the St Theresa mission. You can see that it is situated just here within walking distance. The mission driver, John, is a ZANC member. Make contact with him and he will help you to get back to Mikomfwa."

Wadi Halfa

Tom was up early in the morning and went out onto the deck where he leaned on the rail to watch the sunrise. He admired a tiny fennec that was sitting on the bank. The slender desert fox was completely unafraid and sat there returning the compliment and gazing at him.

The squad had just finished breakfast and were enjoying a coffee on the hotel veranda when they were joined by the pilot, Mike Wilmot. "Good morning, chaps, I've been out to the airstrip. The mechanics say they have almost finished work on the plane and we should be on our way in less than two hours. It's a short hop from here to Khartoum, and then we will carry on to Entebbe on Lake Victoria where we have an overnight stop. I'm sure you will enjoy that hotel, it is a big improvement on this one, the grounds are lush, it has a big swimming pool and it sits right on the shores of the lake."

"There's every chance that the hippos will put on a moonlight serenade for you and I'm sure you will enjoy the ice-cold Tusker beer."

The landing at Khartoum came and went in a flash, there was probably mail to be dropped-off or collected but it was almost literally a case of touch and go.

When Tom next looked out of the window, he thought he must have dozed for a while because the scenery below had changed dramatically. Mile after boring mile of rocks and sand had been replaced by scrubby bush.

Then by rolling savannah grasslands, stands of trees, clusters of thatched huts and herds of cattle.

"Welcome back! You pack quite a snore, Tom, but I can tell you that you didn't miss much. However, it's finally beginning to look more interesting down below. I figure that we are probably looking at Southern Sudan since I shouldn't think we are as far south as Uganda yet. We could either ask Joan to check our location with Mike or we can amuse ourselves by looking for clues."

Tom said, "Well, it's suddenly become a very intense green down there and I can see plenty of glints where bodies of water are catching the sun so my guess would be that we are flying over the Sudd."

"I've heard the term before, but perhaps you can explain to me what exactly is 'The Sudd', Tom?"

"The Sudd is a section of the White Nile that lies in South Central Sudan, Rob. The fact that it is probably one of the world largest wetlands means that it is of great ecological importance. In effect, it is a natural dam composed of a vast build-up of papyrus, water hyacinth and aquatic grasses. It acts like an immense sponge that blocks and controls the flow of the river. The region has always fascinated me because I believe the bird-life there is phenomenal."

"Does that mean that you are a 'birder', Tom?"

"That's for sure, and I'm hoping I may have a chance to spot one or two 'lifers' when we reach Lake Victoria this afternoon."

"Rob!" Tom was excitedly poking Rob's shoulder, "Look down there, can you see that elephant?"

"Got him, Tom, it's odd that he looks sort of two-tone."

"I think he's halfway through a clean-up, Rob and he still needs to wash the dust off his back."

"Did I hear you guys say you've just seen an elephant?" Pat asked. "I wish I'd seen that, but I guess, we will get to see plenty of them in Northern Rhodesia."

Tom continued to look out of the window and caught tantalising glimpses of various antelope until they began to descend and Joan came on the intercom.

"Ladies and gentlemen, we are approaching the Entebbe Airport, please fasten your seatbelts. Transport will be waiting to take you to the Lake Hotel where I am sure you would all like to enjoy a swim. The hotel shuttle passed through a pair of imposing gates to enter into the extensive grounds of the Lake Hotel."

Tom pointed to a mass of flowering shrubs. "Do you see how many birds there are feeding on those bushes, Rob; they mostly drink the nectar from the flowers although some catch insects."

"Would that mean that they are humming birds, Tom?"

"Nice try, Rob, but no, they are not humming birds, they are sunbirds, the African equivalent of the New World humming birds. They are very small and colourful but not as tiny as humming birds and they can't fly backwards. I'm going to do a quick couple of lengths in the pool then I'll make a tour of the gardens to check the birds, do you fancy coming along?"

"I think I'll give that a miss, thanks, Tom. The birds that I want to check will probably be sitting around the pool."

Sundowner drinks and snacks were served on the terrace looking out over the lake. Tom found Rob, Pat and Jack savouring the first Tusker beers of the evening. "What, no company, chaps, does that mean the poolside birding was not so good?"

"Truth be told, Tom, the talent was a bit thin on the ground, but who knows it's still early and maybe it will improve later on."

"How did your birding go?" Rob asked.

"It was really incredible thanks, Rob; I clocked a whole string of 'lifers'."

"Maybe you could enlighten me, Tom, what constitutes a 'lifer' in your jargon?" Pat asked.

"Most serious birders keep a life-list, Pat, in other words, a list of all the birds they have seen and positively identified in their entire lifetime. When you see and positively identify a bird for the first time, you can add it to your list. Then for you that is a 'lifer'."

A huge bellow made them all sit up and look out at the lake. The waiter bringing the next round of Tuskers laughed and said, "You need not worry, sirs, that's just one of the hippos tuning up for the evening serenade. However, I should mention that you are requested not to walk on the lakeside lawns after dark. That is when the hippos come out onto the grass. They are aggressive animals; they can be very dangerous and they are surprisingly fast. You should be warned that it is not possible for a man to outrun a hippo. The crocs may also come up onto the lawn at times but it's the hippos that are the real danger."

By this time, the other members of the chorus had arrived and they were treated to a cacophony of sound.

In the shallows at the edge of the lake, the big bulls opened their jaws wide, flashed their huge tushes, roared and tried to intimidate one another. They eventually settled down as the sunset hues intensified, the light faded and preceded by the planet Venus, the stars began to show.

The milky-way cast a swathe across the sky and the lights were subdued on the lake side of the hotel to allow the guests to enjoy the full wonder of the African night.

A drumbeat signalled that it was time for dinner. The main course was a mutton curry with freshly-ground East African spices. It was incredible and a message of complements to the chef was universally approved.

After dinner, the dance floor was cleared and a quartet took the stage.

The members of the aircrew were seated close by and on hearing them open with a slow-foxtrot; Tom went over to ask Joan Grey if she would dance with him.

They had the floor to themselves, quickly found a rhythm and were soon dancing well together.

Then floor began to fill. Tom saw that Rob was dancing with Jean Milner (the bride to be) and Jack was dancing with an attractive girl who was laughing at something he had said. The rhythm changed to a waltz as Tom led Joan back to her table and Pat was there in a flash.

Before she could sit, he had taken her hand and led her onto the floor for back to back waltzes.

Then the opening notes of a tango rapidly cleared the floor. Much to everyone's surprise, the quiet guardsman Ivor stood up and went over to Joan.

"You dance very well, what do you think, shall we show them how it's done?"

She smiled and said, "Why not?" So they did. It was obvious that Joan was an accomplished dancer and Ivor performed very creditably. When the music stopped they took their bows to an enthusiastic round of applause. Back at the table, Ivor was greeted by Rob with, "I thought the marines had it, Ivor, but you've just taken the wind out of our sails, you really are a dark horse." Between the dancing and more Tuskers, it was a late night.

Tom was still up at first light and down at the lake shore. He watched the birds fishing and marvelled at their various techniques.

Several species of kingfisher were 'still-hunting' meaning that they perched high on a branch then plunged into the water from their vantage point to catch their prey. The small black and white, pied kingfishers on the other hand hovered in mid-air then closed their wings to dive into the water. The cormorants and African darters or 'snake birds' finned around on the surface then ducked below to hunt shoals of fish.

Thc herons and egrets stalked around in the shallows until they found a position, then they stood incredibly still and waited for a fish or frog to come within striking distance of their bill. He saw a hamerkop; it was a large plain brown bird with a strange wedge shaped head. It shuffled its feet and danced in the shallow water to disturb any small fish or amphibians that were hiding in the mud then it caught them with a quick lunge of its head. High up in a dead tree at the waters' edge he saw a fish eagle patiently watching all this activity. It eventually launched itself into a long glide, accelerating as it neared the water, then dropped its legs and opened its needle-sharp clawed feet wide to strike a large fish that was cruising close to the surface.

The eagle flapped its wings strongly as it took the weight, to avoid entering the water. Then it carried the fish back up to its perch where it settled down to enjoy its breakfast.

Tom decided his birding time was up when he heard a lively tune played on the marimba.

He headed back to the hotel thinking, that must be the call for the guests to come to breakfast. After a sumptuous buffet breakfast, the shuttle took the passengers to the airport where the ground staff immediately started to load their luggage. Joe was there to make sure that the luggage for those passengers going all the way to Salisbury was stowed at the back of the hold and Joan was at the foot of the ramp to see them onto the plane.

Everything went smoothly and once they had attained cruising altitude; Mike came over on the intercom. "Good morning, ladies and gentlemen, today we will be making two landings in Northern Rhodesia where the weather is fine and sunny. There are two of you who are to disembark when we land in Ndola, and then when we reach Lusaka, the fourteen members of the Northern Rhodesian Police contingent will be leaving us. To all our passengers, I would like to take this opportunity to say that it has been a pleasure to have you fly with us and I hope that the future will see you repeat the experience of flying with Central African Airways."

Lusaka

At the Lusaka Airport, the members of the NRP squad bade farewell to the other passengers and thanked the aircrew for the excellent attention they had received during the long flight. Then, their passports stamped and their work permits checked, they boarded a police bus that was waiting to take them to the NRP training school at Lilayi. The fleeting impression that they gained during their quick passage through Lusaka conjured up images of the American wild-west, with dirt roads, boardwalks, and saloons with bat-wing doors.

Lilayi, that lay a relatively short distance to the south-east of town, had the appearance of a typical army barracks.

The bus rolled to a halt on the edge of a huge parade ground. The squad members had just begun to off-load their luggage when a stentorian voice ordered them to 'ground your kit and fall in'.

A short thick-set man with the three silver bars of a chief inspector on his shoulders and the voice of a drill sergeant was marching towards them across the parade ground.

He carried a pace-stick tucked rigidly under his arm. "Att-en-shun, oh my god, I don't believe my eyes, do I really see no less than four marines! Gentlemen, you had better know that I am Chief Inspector Brown and I intend to make you suffer. You can rest assured I'm going to drill that slovenly marine nonsense out of you. Gentlemen, your quarters are on the first floor of the block to your left. Left turn, dismiss."

"Am I just being paranoid or does one get a distinct impression that the chief inspector is not overly fond of marines?" Rob asked.

"Never mind him, Rob, we all know these drill types, he's probably just trying to press our buttons and get us steamed up," said Tom.

Outfitting the members of the new squad with short and long khaki uniforms, dress blues, mess kits, tuxedos, dress shirts, etc., was enough to keep several of the Indian tailors in Lusaka very busy. The chief inspector ensured that acquiring gym gear was made a priority since he wanted every day to begin with an eighteen mile run starting at the crack of dawn.

Much to the chief's chagrin, the marines ran as a group and always came in comfortably ahead of the rest of the squad. "There are four marines in this squad and they are much too full of themselves," he told senior inspector Don Barker, the weapons training instructor.

"I'd like to see them brought down a peg and I'm hoping your first session of small arms training with them tomorrow will help to sort the men from the boys."

Harry Brown knew exactly where he would find Don Barker the following evening.

He was sure to be downing an ice cold Lion lager in the mess after a long day on the range.

He took a seat next to Don at the bar and immediately asked, "So how did it go on the range today?"

"Well, Harry, I had just issued to them with side-arms, so I decided to start with those before taking them out to the main range. They fired on figure targets from ten, fifteen and twenty yards. The first three places were taken by Auld, Savage and O'Brian with Frost a close fourth."

"How can that be, Don! You mean to say that the marines took the first four places. What about the army men, especially the guards!"

"There's no denying the guards were good, Harry, but they weren't good enough. It was exactly the same story out on the range with the Sterling. However, the guardsman Price did take second place at both two hundred and three hundred yards with the Lee Enfield rifle. There's no doubt that those marines have been well trained, in fact, I'd say you'll find it hard to fault them in the use of weapons."

"I did overhear O'Brian trying to assure the other marines that horse-riding is no more difficult than riding a bike so they are definitely concerned about equitation. It should be interesting to see how they fare when Mac introduces them to their mounts tomorrow."

"Good morning, gentlemen. I am Senior Inspector MacArthur your equitation instructor. I realise that you must be sad to have missed your morning jog, but never mind, you will still have the opportunity to explore the neighbouring countryside from a different viewpoint. I can promise you that you will have a much better view once you're mounted on one of our friends here."

"The program is as follows. We will begin with a quiet hack for a couple of miles to give you and your mount the opportunity to get to get to know one another. You will find that you have some work to do since your mount will inevitably try to take control and you must make it clear that it is you who is boss."

"We will eventually make our way to the wildlife orphanage at Chilanga where we are going to pay a visit to Joy Adamson. Joy is quite famous and I wonder if any of you have heard of her?"

"Yes, O'Brian, isn't it? What have you heard?"

"Isn't Mrs Adamson the Lion Lady? I read a book called *Born Free* about her and her husband George, but I thought they lived in Kenya?"

"That's true, they were in Kenya at that time but they divorced and Joy has moved down here to take over at Chilanga. As you say, O'Brian, Mrs Adamson is the 'Lion Lady' and she has put together quite a collection of feline orphans in addition to other orphaned or injured wildlife at the orphanage."

The horses obviously knew the drill since they were already becoming fractious before the group reached Chilanga.

Mac told the squad they must make sure that their mounts were securely tied to a hitching rail just inside the gates before he took them to meet Joy. The cat smell from the enclosures that housed sleeping lions was very strong.

They passed a wide-awake caracal that hissed and spat furiously at them.

When they found Joy, she was in one of the larger enclosures playing with a magnificent leopard. She gave the cat a final hug before coming out to greet them, locking the gate behind her.

Mac introduced the squad and asked if it would be possible for them to have a short tour. "Certainly, Mac, I would normally ask Daniel to take them, however he's busy preparing meals for the animals so I'll give you a quick walk through myself. You must see my latest addition; it has a beautiful smile. It's not an orphan but when it got into a farm dam, the farmer was going to shoot it. I convinced him it would be better for him to let me trap it." Her treasure was a crocodile more than two metres in length. They admired it as it lay with its mouth wide open displaying an array of needle-sharp teeth.

When they left the orphanage, they rode on to the Blue Boar Inn to sample the latest batch of their draught beer before heading back to training school.

It was Tom's 21st that Saturday, so it was a good excuse to have a party. They played such action games as Bok-Bok, British Bulldog and High Cockalorum interspersed with lots of down-down cocktails. They contained some of everything that was behind the bar and Tom had to down them completely in one gulp.

At some stage in the small hours, the idea that it would be fun to introduce Joy Adamson's crocodile to the new pool at the Ridgeway Hotel came up. No sooner said than done, securely wrapped-up in blankets and carpets, the croc was bundled into the training school bus. It was transported to the Ridgeway where it was released into the swimming pool.

Sunday 'hangover morning' came with a rude awakening. 'Chiefy' came banging on the doors with his pace-stick as he marched down the corridor of the officers' quarters.

"Come on, come on, you young buggers, out you get and fall in on the square. We have received a complaint from the Ridgeway Hotel. You are to go there immediately and remove that crocodile from their pool. If you think that is bad, just wait until Joy Adamson gets hold of you for exposing her precious crocodile to pool chemicals."

On completion of the course, Tom was posted to the Copperbelt and as the latest member of the Luanshya Police Force; he was nominated to take over the role of farm and rural patrols officer. His area of responsibility included a thinly populated native reserve roughly the size of Wales and the numerous small-holdings and farms that bordered on the towns. He felt that this could be to his advantage since it would afford him the opportunity of getting to know the whole district including the vast Lamba-Lima native reserve.

He soon discovered that the Ndola rural district was very wild. He encountered a pride of lions, an elephant wreaking havoc at a huge tomato farm and a leopard that was preying on farmer's dogs, in addition to herds of a wide variety of game animals. That was all during his first week of policing the area.

Early one morning, he received a call from the neighbour of a Mrs Dodds. She was calling on Mrs Dodds her behalf because there was no telephone on the Dodd's farm. "You are needed to come out here urgently inspector, it seems that there has been a fatal accident."

He recalled that a widow named Dodds owned the farm. She had a number of sons, a couple of scrawny cows, half a dozen virtually wild pigs, some goats and chickens. The sons did very little to help their mother provide for the family, other than catching some fish from the big dam on the property.

While the Dodds had quite a big block of land, they had never made any real attempt to farm it.

Their staff grew mealies, masaka, nyauti, cassava and some 'dagga' (marijuana) on ground that they worked next to their quarters.

Mrs Dodds boys were virtually wild and they often entertained themselves by playing 'Cowboys and Indians'.

The younger boys were made to play the part of 'Indians'. They were sent off into the bush with makeshift bows and arrows. Then the older 'cowboys' followed and hunted them with air-rifles. Fortunately, it was usually imaginative play because the boys rarely got into town and when they did they seldom had money to buy pellets. However this practice did constitute an accident waiting to happen.

In fact, it was almost inevitable that an occasion would arise when the rural patrol officer would have to go out there to investigate an incident.

When Tom got to the farm, he found that one of the 'Redskins' had been fatally wounded.

The weapons the boys were using were of a small calibre, but a 0.22 air-rifle pellet can still be lethal. Especially as in this instance where one had entered through the eye and penetrated the brain. Tom questioned Mrs Dodds and several of the boys, opened a file and filled out report.

He submitted these details to CID and requested that they follow up on the case.

The eldest youngster, who had fired the fatal shot, was eighteen and there was a possibility that he may have to face a charge. However, the CID team determined that the incident should simply be written off as a hunting accident.

The Dodds family largely subsisted on the barbel they caught and the mother either pickled or dried.

The odd sheep or goat that they stole from their neighbours probably served to provide them with a change of diet.

They had two old tin boats for hire. A broad-beamed dingy that was ideal for fishing and a long slender canoe that was fast but unstable.

It was only used by the more adventurous spirits.

One Saturday morning, when a good many people were either fishing or picnicking at the Dodds dam, a young girl in her early teens was taken by a crocodile. Tom Savage was out on farm patrol visiting the more westerly small-holdings when he received a radio message about the attack. He immediately put foot and arrived on site in less than thirty minutes.

He sent Constable Kafwembe to check if the staff or any of their family had witnessed the incident or if they were aware of a large crocodile that had moved into the dam. Meanwhile, he went to question the fishermen and picnickers.

As is invariably the case with eye-witnesses, he received very contradictory accounts. However, in broad terms, the witnesses could be placed into two categories. There were those who stated that they had seen an absolutely enormous crocodile attack the boat, capsize it and carry off the girl.

The second group consisted mainly of the fishermen, who said that the canoe was notoriously unstable. It capsized and the girl had been swimming back to the bank when a big crocodile came and took her.

This group was more consistent even giving Tom a rough indication of where the attack took place. Sadly, he knew that there was very little hope of finding the girl alive.

She would have drowned while she was being carried off. The croc must have taken her under water for quite some distance in order to reach a place where it could have established its lair.

Kafwembe came to report and stated that he had failed to find anyone who had seen the attack. However, several of the staff told him that they were aware of the presence of a very large crocodile in the river.

They believed that it had made itself at home in the upper reaches of the dam where the river was choked with drowned trees.

A rapid examination of the topography convinced Tom that they would need to access the area of the upper dam and feeder river from the water.

He went back to the farm patrols Land Rover to make a report to Luanshya Central over the radio and to collect his rifle and binoculars.

Having commandeered the more stable boat, they set off. Kafwembe plied the paddle while Tom scanned the banks as they moved slowly up the dam and into the river. This had been a valley of dense riverine bush before the dam was built.

Now, there were numerous dead hardwood trees standing in place, that had been drowned by the rising water.

Once they had moved some distance up the river, they paused against one of the dead trees. Tom spent a few minutes examining a large bed for any indication that a passage may have been forced through the reeds.

They were both so totally focussed on finding any evidence of the presence of a large crocodile that they were totally unaware of the thousands of fire ants that were boarding the boat.

It is uncanny how red ants can swarm all over their victim without being detected then pass a mysterious signal that enables them all to bite simultaneously. The sensation is one of suddenly being jabbed with thousands of red hot needles.

When that happened, they didn't give the crocodile a second thought and they both jumped out of the boat in a flash! As they waded ashore, they grabbed handfuls of the sticky black mud to rub themselves down with and try to peel-off the ants.

Meantime, the boat with its load of ants had drifted away heading off down river.

They were left to force their way painfully through the bush with soaking wet clothes and their boots rubbing on thousands of ant bites. It was heavy going battling through the dense growth of the river valley. It was long after dark when they eventually got back to the aged and battered, short-wheel base, farm patrols Land Rover.

When they got back to the station, Tom sent Kafwembe off to his quarters, with a warning that he must be prepared for an early start in the morning. He logged a brief entry in the occurrence book then walked to the mess. He got there to find and eat the dried out meal Lou Spencer, the house keeper, had kindly placed in the fridge for him.

Then he sat and wrote his report over a hard earned cup of coffee.

Back at his quarters when he switched on the light, 'Jade' his bright green praying mantis flew straight onto the blotting pad on his desk. She raised her forelegs in a challenge to let him know that she was ready for their traditional evening 'boxing match.'

Although Tom was feeling rather tired, he couldn't let her down so they sparred for a while, her two forelegs against his two fingers. Perhaps she could sense that his heart wasn't in it, so after a couple of minutes, she flew up to the ceiling cornice where she got stuck into her real job of polishing off the 'mozzies.' She was ably helped in this project by a young gecko 'James' who had adopted him (or vice-versa). James was thriving on a diet of the numerous insects that were attracted by Tom's light when he worked late studying for the law exams.

A thump on the wall let him know that Bill Sharp was 'at home'. Bill was his next-door neighbour and they went way back a long way.

In fact, it was because of Bill that he was in Northern Rhodesia. They had served together in 45 Royal Marines Commando in Cyprus, Suez, Libya and Malta. Bill had suggested that they should join the colonial police after they were demobbed.

Bill had a girl in every port. If you ever saw the TV series the 'A' team then you would only need to think of the character 'Face' to have an image of Bill Sharp in both appearance and nature.

Tom was up way ahead of the sparrows the following morning and walked over to book in at the charge office where Kafwembe was already waiting. Then they went down to the motor pool to collect the Land Rover.

It was all gassed-up and checked out ready for them so they were soon on the road. As they headed out of town, they disturbed Natal nightjars crouched on the road and bush-babies high up in the bush with their bright red eyes. Pennant-winged nightjars their streamer feathers fluttering, danced in the headlights and hares trapped in their headlights zigzagged ahead of them. Tom had to slow down for a honey-badger and they watched him cross the road muttering under his breath at their impertinence of interfering with his night's hunting.

When they reached the main Ndola-Kitwe road at Fisenge, they turned west towards Kitwe-Nkana. Then at the second road bridge, they turned north onto the farm track that led to the Dodds farm.

Tom parked under a tree near the farmhouse and went to see Mrs Dodds. When he had previously visited on farm patrol, he had always dealt with the boys so he had still to meet their mother.

He knocked on the front door and she shouted to tell him that he must come around the back as she was in the kitchen.

She opened the back door and he saw that she was skinny, wrinkled and grey, obviously worn to a thread, like her dress. Her eyes were also grey but bright and they still held a spark of humour.

He knew that she was probably in her late fifties or early sixties but she looked like an octogenarian.

Tom apologised to her, explaining that under the circumstances that had prevailed on the previous day, it had not been possible to get her permission before taking out a boat.

She said she quite understood the urgency he had felt to find and deal with a man-eating crocodile.

"You must at least sit down for a minute, Inspector Savage and tell me a little of what is happening because I haven't been to town in years." She poured him a cup of coffee from the pot that was on the Aga stove then filled a mug, adding plenty of sugar, to take out to Kafwembe who was sitting in the yard.

"Well, I'm based in Luanshya so there is usually very little to report, Mrs Dodds. Life in our small town is generally quite quiet when compared to Ndola and Kitwe. I'm sure you must know Mrs Uys, Dirk Uys' widow? I met her walking to town when we were on our way here this morning."

"I stopped for a brief chat. She is over ninety now but she still walks the seven miles from her plot into Luanshya at least once a week. She always likes to start out in the small hours when it's still nice and cool."

"Yes indeed, I remember Granny Uys, so she is still going strong! When my husband was alive, he used to drive us over now and then to have tea with her. Inspector, my staff have been talking a great deal about a new church, what can you tell me about that?"

"I am sure they must be speaking of the Lumpa Church. It is a version of faith that combines Catholicism and Animism and it has become quite strong in the townships. It is apolitical and that has caused quite a stir because the converts believe that they are protected from witch-craft. They staunchly refuse to ally themselves to any political party, to recognise any earthly authority or to pay taxes. The movement was started by a woman from Chinsali called Alice Lenshina."

"Her background is that she became comatose as the result of suffering from cerebral malaria. When she recovered and came out of the coma, she stated that while she was unconscious, she had met with Jesus Christ who had given her an apostolic mission. She certainly has charisma and she has rapidly attracted a substantial following."

"There have already been a number of clashes between Lumpa Church congregations and the one party state UNIP political activists." The Lumpas have built fortified villages to protect themselves from UNIP attacks.

"Well, many thanks for the coffee, Mrs Dodds, but its high time Kafwembe and I got after that crocodile."

"You must ask one of the older boys if you need to use a boat today inspector. They will know if either of the boats are booked or have been holed. I must tell you that we get some wild youngsters coming out to the dam to party and all too often they end up damaging our boats."

There were no prior bookings for the boats, so they were soon on their way heading up the dam and into the river.

There were dense beds of tall reeds on both banks once they entered the feeder river and they were obliged to move slowly examining them carefully. They must have travelled about half a mile when they reached a point where the river was too blocked by dead and fallen trees for them to make any progress. Tom decided to cut across and try to find a course closer to the opposite side.

He hoped that with the change of direction and tack, they may spot some clue regarding the activities of the crocodile.

They had made slow progress and it was some hours before they turned and made their way back down river and into the dam having met with a total lack of success.

Tom told Kafwembe, “I’m afraid it looks as if this calls for a night hunt. We will have to go back to Central, have a bite to eat, change our gear, collect two bulalla lights and come back after dark. Hopefully, the crocodile will be bolder to come out into the open water after dark and we may pick up his eyes.”

When they got back out to the farm that evening, Tom was dismayed to learn that one of the Dodds boys had decided to try to catch a barbel using the steadier boat and had managed to hole it by ramming it into a jagged rock.

Kafwembe looking doubtfully at the slender canoe and said, “Sir, it will be very dangerous to go after that big crocodile in this useless boat.”

Tom told him, “I know that, Kafwembe, but we don’t have a choice, this is the only boat and it is very important that we get that croc as soon as possible before it is responsible for more deaths. It is a great danger to any of the numerous families who come to here to swim or fish from the bank. Coming from Lake Mweru, I take it that you can swim?”

“Of course, I can swim, Bwana!” Kafwembe said indignantly.

As they headed out cautiously across the dam, Tom picked up several pairs of glowing cigarette-end eyes with the light. They were small and close together so definitely not big crocs.

Then as they entered the river, they began to pick up the eyes of more sizeable specimens but they were still much too small for the killer. They were about quarter of a mile up the river when Tom caught a glimpse of something on the bank, through a narrow gap in a bed of reeds.

Tom held up an open hand against the light to signal Kafwembe to stop and he focussed his light through the gap. He could see the back legs and the beginnings of the crested tail of a huge croc. He thought, *I may not have the opportunity of another shot before this croc kills again so I have to make the most of this chance.*

He targeted the area where the crocodile's pelvis met his spine since he knew that the hard-nosed 303 bullet would need to hit bone if it was to do any serious damage. Otherwise the bullet would just pass straight through leaving a clean flesh wound.

Tom told Kafwembe to keep his light on the croc and to do his best to hold the boat steady.

However, when Tom took the shot, Kafwembe was so startled that he lost control and capsized the boat tipping them both into the river. The boat sank like a stone as they heard the croc thrashing about in the reeds then there was a loud splash as he hit the water.

Once again, they found themselves wading through deep mud and dense reeds to reach the bank.

Tom said, "We will have to come back here again tomorrow. You must ask Sgt Phiri to lend us a length of rope that you can bring along. We will attach it to the canoe and that will make it easier to pull it out. Hopefully, we will find that the spare clip of ammunition and any other stuff we had is still in the boat. Once we have daylight, we will be able to read any signs left by the crocodile."

"Meanwhile, we had better get going, it will take us at least an hour to get back to the vehicle, it's already late and we will have to make another early start in the morning."

Tom was having coffee with Mrs Dodds the following morning when one of her sons came to tell them that he had patched the second boat. "That's grand," Tom said, "I suggest Kafwembe and I take this boat up to the top end of the dam, pull out and empty the canoe then bring them both back? While we are up there, we will have a good look around and try to find any evidence that may have been left by the croc I wounded."

They ran the boat ashore just down river from the reed-bed where they had encountered the crocodile. They walked along the sand bank until they reached the site. They could immediately see where the croc had thrashed around, bled and voided itself, then pushed through the reeds to the water.

"Look here, sir," said Kafwembe pointing to deep footprints in the sand. "You can see that this is where the croc lifted himself up onto his front legs. Here you can see that he had to drag his back legs. He was too damaged to use them."

"I think your shot must either have shattered his pelvis or broken his spine. With an injury like that, a crocodile will always try to reach his lair so that he can lie down and die quietly."

It seems that Kafwembe's reading of the situation must have been correct because nothing further was ever heard of that huge Dodds' crocodile.

Badger's But

Tom came into his office after inspecting the day shift to be greeted by the switchboard operator with, "Good morning, sir, there's a call on line 2 for you."

“Good morning, Inspector Savage, it’s Will Priestly here, from the Badger’s But poultry farm out at Fisenge. You may remember paying us a visit some weeks ago during one of your farm patrols.”

“Of course, Mr Priestly, and once again many thanks for your hospitality.”

“It was our pleasure, inspector, but I wonder if I may ask a favour of you?”

“Certainly, please call me Tom and tell me how I may be of assistance?”

“Well Tom, I’m sure you are aware that petty theft of such minor items as sugar, salt, bread, biscuits and even the odd tin of food has to be taken as a simple fact of life in this part of the world. However, of late, the extent of the theft taking place on our farm is getting out of hand.”

“My wife recalled that during your visit to us, you mentioned that the Lamba-Lima tribal trust lands fall within your area of responsibility. That has prompted her to suggest that you may know of a powerful *nganga* (witchdoctor) capable of casting a spell that would put the fear of god into anyone stealing from this farm. Do you think such a thing is possible?”

“I do frequently encounter cases involving witchcraft especially in the tribal lands though it’s not as uncommon as you might think on the farms or even in town. However, as you are no doubt aware, Will, witchcraft is only as powerful as a person’s belief in it.”

That said, it is true that our rural people are very superstitious.

“I have frequently seen evidence of the strong hold that the chief’s *nganga* has over them. If you wish, I can ask the chief for permission to bring his witchdoctor out to Badger's But."

"However, before I approach him on this matter you must assure me that: A. this is something you really want to get involved with and: B. you are prepared to accept the outcome of this action, whatever that may be?"

"Yes indeed, Tom, I quite understand but my wife is set on this course of action so would you please be kind enough to go ahead and do this for us as soon as possible."

Tom put down the phone and dispatched a constable with an instruction for Sgt Zulu to report to his office.

"Good morning, Sgt Zulu, I understand that Constable Kafwembe is making good progress with his language studies?"

"Yes indeed, sir, Sgt Mbambala, our linguist informs me that he already has quite a good understanding of the local language. In fact, he should soon be able to qualify for a language supplement to his pay. Of course, Kafwembe is fortunate in that the chiLamba that is spoken here is closely related to his home language of chiBemba."

"That is excellent news; please tell him that he must report to me in the vehicle park at 6:00am tomorrow morning. He will have an opportunity to practice his chiLamba since I am going to pay Chief Nkana a visit."

Tom knew and admired Chief Nkana both for his depth of understanding of his people and for the skilful way in which he frequently managed to resolve their problems.

Always eager to learn more about the life and customs of these people, Tom would frequently sit with the chief as he held court. The chief returned Tom's respect and they enjoyed a cordial relationship.

Tom had already booked out a short-wheel-based Land Rover from the motor pool so they were able to get off to an early start the following morning. The little town with its grid of tarmac roads was quickly left behind.

They splashed through deep pools in low lying spots where the narrow track still held water.

Free of dust the air was cool, clear and fresh. The bush was dense and verdant, flourishing in response to the rains and game was not easy to spot. When they did eventually come upon a more open area on the crest of a rise, Tom stopped to watch some frisky impala.

Their coats were a warm reddish-brown and they were in the peak of condition. It was a small bachelor herd and the young rams had paired-off to spar. They danced around one another, manoeuvring for position, making lunges and repeatedly clashing horns.

These young males were practising, preparing themselves as would be contenders. Their internal clocks were set for the time that would inevitably come when they must challenge an established Alpha ram if they were ever to possess a harem of their own.

A little further on, they came across a breeding herd. It was difficult to count the animals as they moved amongst the trees but there must have been forty to fifty elegant ewes and numerous spindly-legged lambs. The herd was watched over by a magnificent ram. His large lyre-shaped horns bore the extra twist that was still to be acquired by the young bachelors.

Then Tom spotted a flock of splendid glossy starlings perched on dead branch close to the track. He stopped and took out the small pair of roof-prism binoculars that he kept below the dash.

He had barely managed to focus on the birds when they took off, the metallic blues and greens of their wings creating vivid flashes of colour in the sunlight.

"Don't you think those birds were really beautiful?" Tom asked.

"I don't think they are good to eat, sir," Kafwembe replied.

As Tom drove on, it occurred to him that he knew very little of Kafwembe's background other than the simple facts that he was Bemba by tribe and his performance at the Lilayi police training school had been rated as above average.

"I know you are from the Northern Province but that is a really huge area Kafwembe, so tell me where exactly is your home?"

"I am from the south-east side of Lake Mweru, sir. It is right on the border in fact the western side of the lake lies within the Belgian Congo. My father is headman of a small village that sits on an island in the lake. Our main occupation there is fishing. We catch masses of *mandefu*, our name for the whiskered black barbel."

"But you live in such a remote area and fish tends to go off very quickly. If you catch so many, how do you manage to take them to sell on the bigger markets?"

"You see, sir, we build big raised drying platforms. When the fish have been gutted, they are taken up onto the platforms where they are twisted into coils and sun dried. When they have completely dried out, they are taken over to the mainland where they are loaded onto trucks and sent to be sold in the markets on the Copperbelt."

Tom recalled seeing coils of dried barbel for sale on the stalls in the Mikomfwa market but it had not occurred to him that they may have originated from such a distant source.

Kafwembe carried on to say, “We also catch a lot of makumba (bream-tilapia). Those we scale, gut and split before hanging them to dry on wooden racks. They are also bagged to be sold on the Copperbelt but they do not enjoy as much demand as the barbel.”

“I must say your English is very good, Kafwembe. Is that because there is a school on your island where they teach English?”

“No, sir, we do not have a proper school or even a clinic on the island. There is a nursery school for the very small children. After that, the boys who are to have further schooling must leave home to go to one of the schools in Kasama. It is not possible for them all to do that because it is expensive.”

“The girls just work at home, helping their mothers to keep house, tending the crops and gathering wild herbs and fruit. They also fish for the small silvery fish that are plentiful in the shallows of the lake. They are about the size of my finger, make excellent relish and are easy to catch if you use a very small hook and tiny balls of stiff porridge as bait.”

“What about crocs, I would imagine they are plentiful. Surely, girls who are fishing at the edge of the lake must be afraid of them?”

“It’s true, sir, there are many crocodiles, but they are seldom hungry because the black barbel are plentiful and that is their favourite food.

There have been times when a child has been taken but that is very unusual.”

"I notice that many of the people here in the Lamba-Lima have begun planting American maize as a crop, do you find that it is also being used in the north?"

"It has been quite some time since I visited my home but I do not think so, sir. My people are very traditional. They feel happier growing sorgum, cassava, masaka and nauti since those are crops that will always give some yield even in a season when there is hardly any rain."

"May I ask you a question now, sir? Are we really going to transport a witchdoctor to that chicken farm? I am not very superstitious but I must confess that the thought of him travelling in this vehicle with us makes me feel nervous."

"Yes, Kafwembe, the plan is to take a witchdoctor to the Priestly's, but you mustn't worry about it. You see inside all that regalia there is just an ordinary man exactly the same as you and me."

The condition of the gravel roads had been fairly good up to now, despite the heavy rain that had fallen during the night, and they were making good time.

However, Tom had to admit that he was feeling concerned about the condition of the frail bridge they must use to cross the Kafubu River.

When they got there, he was relieved to find that, although the river was flowing strongly and had risen over its banks, the wooden bridge was still passable and appeared to be holding its own against the flood waters.

The chief came out to greet them when they arrived at the village. Chief Nkana's beard was grey and his hair was now completely white. He moved slowly and stiffly, clear evidence of his advancing years.

When they first met, he had told Tom that he did not know his exact age.

Seeing him now Tom estimated that he must be nearly seventy. That was quite a good age in this area where the average life span was less than fifty years.

The chief suggested that Kafwembe should go and join a group of the village elders where they were sitting close by in the shade of a huge mahogany tree. They were sharing a bucket of moa (beer) and enjoying lengthy discussions about a projected hunt. This was an established tradition and it provided an excuse for sitting around and enjoying the beer. The traditional hunt consisted of creating a line of fires with men shouting and waving spears to fill the gaps.

Then when the game panicked, they were driven over the edge of a cliff. Sometimes there was so much meat that other villages were invited to come and help to eat it. The practice was so wasteful that it had been banned by the district commissioner some years ago. The truth being that few could remember the last time that such a major hunt had actually taken place.

The chief asked Tom to join him where one of his wives had placed two chairs outside the big hut. She had also brought a small table intricately carved from a single piece of wood, two mugs of the native beer made from fermented masaka and a wooden bowl of roasted ground nuts.

"It is a long time since I made the journey to Lusaka to attend the council of chiefs. Out here, we know nothing of the world in general.

Please tell me a little of the news, Inspector Savage. I would like to have some idea of what is happening out there?"

"What I must tell you, chief, is that we are living in very troubled times, especially with regard to politics. While Harry Nkumbula is a rock, maintaining his stance as a moderate and holding on to his belief that slow and steady wins the race, Simon Kapwepwe is a firebrand."

"Not only does he constantly make unreasonable demands but he expects to have them fulfilled here and now. Kapwepwe is busy driving a rift through Nkumbula's NRANC. He has already won the support of the Losi brothers Arthur and Simon Wina. It seems likely that Kenneth Kaunda, currently the secretary general of NRANC, will also transfer his loyalty and join the younger men in forming a new party that they intend to name the ZANC. They have already declared their intention of renaming this country Zambia."

"So you tell me that there are new political parties and there may even be a new name for our country! Please slow down and drink some beer, inspector. This is a great deal for an old man like me to assimilate. Can it be possible that the world is changing so quickly and has already changed so much?

Yet out here we are completely unaware of it?"

The chief readily agreed to grant the loan of his witchdoctor. He pointed out that the nganga would probably demand a chicken from the farmer as payment for his services. Tom said he was sure that wouldn't be a problem since Priestly owned a poultry farm.

Back in Luanshya, Tom called Will Priestly. "Right, Will, I've seen the chief and it's all arranged. I'll collect the nganga early the day after tomorrow and bring him straight out to the farm. I must tell you that he's probably going to ask for a chicken in payment for his services. I've seen him perform and I can assure you he will put on a good show. He certainly always looks very imposing when he's rigged-out in his full regalia to attend the chief's court."

Ufiti (Witchcraft)

"Well, hello there! What's your problem 'blue', did you wet the bed? I take it you must know it's scarcely 4:00 in the morning?" The officer in charge of the night shift was Jim Auld. Sandy haired and grey-eyed there was something about Jim that gave him away as a Scot before he spoke a single word.

Tom and Jim went back a long way. They had first met and bonded playing rugby for 45 Commando Royal Marines during their national service.

With Jim at scrum half to Tom's fly-half they made a devastating pair that had swept all before them in the Near and Middle East Sevens Championships.

"It's going to be a long day; Jim and I need to get an early start. Has Constable Kafwembe checked in yet?"

"Yes, he came in here about ten minutes ago. You'll find him outside waiting by the vehicle."

"Thanks, Jim, and cheers for now, maybe we'll have a chance to catch up later on in the mess."

"Good luck and by the way, Tom, you may need it. I hear you are going to be encountering some *ufiti* today."

The night was pitch-black as they set off. The sky completely overcast with no moon or stars to lighten the darkness.

The headlights picked up a bright red bead of light on the track that proved to be the eye of a pennant-winged nightjar.

The bird launched itself into the air its outer wing feathers trailing behind it as long streamers. Tom thought, *That was quite a sight, but if I were to mention it to Kafwembe, I know he's only going to tell me 'it is not good to eat.' Come to think of it he's probably quite right.*

A spring-hare suddenly bobbed-up almost under the wheels of the vehicle.

Trapped in the glare of the headlights, it kept pace with them for quite a few bounds, looking for all-the-world like a miniature kangaroo.

Then with a flirt of its long black-tipped tail, it changed direction, escaped the headlights and disappeared into the bush.

"Did you see that spring-hare, Kafwembe?"

"Yes, I did see that animal, sir. I don't know your name for it but I do know that it is good to eat."

The silvery-grey streamers of a false dawn were just beginning to lighten the sky as they reached the Kafubu.

The river was still over its banks but the water level had dropped and Tom was glad to find that the bridge was still standing. He sent Kafwembe on ahead explaining how he must set about checking that the decking was still secure.

When Kafwembe reached the far side and waved him on, he carefully eased the vehicle across.

The rain had cut deep gulleys into the steep track that led down to the river on this bank. Tom was kept so busy trying to find a way through this maze that he didn't recognise a tall man standing next to the track wearing a white shirt and black slacks.

"Sir, that man we just passed, he is waving and I think he wants us to stop."

Tom halted the vehicle. "I must say that is a strange way for someone to dress out here, Kafwembe. He looks like an office worker to me so perhaps he needs a lift into town."

As the man approached the vehicle, they saw that he was closely followed by a youngster carrying a large bundle bound-up in a full cow-hide.

"Good morning, inspector, I think you must have come for me."

Tom did a double-take; it was hard to believe that this could be the witchdoctor he had seen at Chief Nkana's court.

"You are obviously surprised, inspector, but then you have only seen me dressed for the court in my full regalia. Surely, you didn't imagine that I would travel around the countryside dressed like that?"

Tom got out to introduce himself, and they shook hands.

The 'nganga' introduced himself as a Lamba chief, named Charles N'gidi.

Once the bulky bundle was disposed of at the rear of the vehicle, they all climbed aboard and got underway.

"So you are in fact a Lamba chief, but how is it that you also came to be a witch doctor?" Tom asked.

Charles told him, "The hereditary post of witch-doctor has been in my family for many years. My father began to train me and pass on the secrets of our trade when I was still a small child. He taught me where to find and how to recognise the many herbs we use. Some, but not all of these herbs can be beneficial, some prevent the subject from being able to lie to me and there are others that can place the subject completely in my power. As I grew older, he also began to teach me how to read and manipulate people, through their expressions and mannerisms. Then when I was at university I studied botany and psychology."

"Well, I have certainly come to the right person," said Tom. "We are going to visit Badger's But, it is a small holding a short distance to the north of Luanshya. The wife of the farmer there complains that they are experiencing an extent of theft by servant that is totally out of hand. She hopes that you can cast a spell so strong that it will make them afraid to steal."

Once they were close to the farm, Tom parked in a quiet loop off the old Ndola Road where Charles would have some privacy to don the regalia that would affect his transformation into a witchdoctor.

This took quite some time but when he finally appeared from behind a dense clump of bushes, Kafwembe could not prevent himself from letting out a gasp.

The n'ganja certainly made an imposing figure with the massive head dress of horn, fur and owls' feathers adding to his already impressive height. The white paste that coated his face gave him a ghostly look.

Charles took off the head dress and handed it to his assistant before climbing into the passenger seat next to Tom.

Kafwembe reluctantly got into the back of the vehicle.

It was a short distance to Badger's But where the gate was opened for them. Tom parked the vehicle under a tree close to the house then went in to greet the Priestlys.

"Come through to the kitchen and have a coffee," Will called. "So, Tom have you brought Lillian her witchdoctor?"

"I certainly have, Will, and he is all primed to put on a show for your staff and farm hands."

“Come through, Lill, Inspector Savage is here and he has brought your secret weapon.”

While they sat in the kitchen having coffee, Tom explained that the witchdoctor would expect to receive a chicken for his services.

“Fair enough, Tom, but you should know that our birds are not ordinary poultry, they are black Australorps and I paid a fortune to import a top class stud rooster from Australia.”

When they went out to the pens, the witchdoctor was studying the birds and immediately indicated that he would need to use the stud rooster in order to cast a strong spell. Will Priestly objected strongly but his wife insisted that he should agree, if that was what was needed, since they already had dozens of youngsters that carried the rooster’s good genes.

The witchdoctor caught the rooster quickly, held it firmly by the neck and bit off and ate its head. Then he began to dance and chant as he made his way to the gate posts.

He made incantations and spattered blood on both gateposts, then he set off clockwise around the property chanting and spattering blood especially on the corner posts. The staff and labour clustered together in the yard watching in silent awe.

As they drove back, Charles explained that he had put a curse on anyone who had stolen, thought of stealing or planned to steal from the farm. He doffed his regalia in the same loop and the journey back to Nkana’s village was uneventful.

Tom received a call from Lillian Priestly the following day. “Inspector Savage, they have all gone, we have no staff or labour. Will went out to see if he could find some of the casual labour that usually hang around looking for jobs but they have all refused to come on the property. We can't operate without staff, so can you please organise to have the curse removed?"

"I'm sorry, Mrs Priestly, but I don't think I can help. In fact, I believe it proves the truth of the old adage, be careful of what you wish for." The fact is that these people are deeply superstitious and going through a routine purporting to remove the curse from the property will not remove the curse from the minds of the people.

Ndola-Lusaka Rail Trolley

As the latest member of the Luanshya Police Force, Tom Savage found that he had been nominated to take over the role of farm and rural patrol officer. His areas of responsibility included a thinly populated native reserve roughly the size of Wales and the numerous small-holdings and farms that bordered on the towns. He decided that this could be to his advantage. It would certainly afford him ample opportunity to get to know the whole district including the vast Lamba-Lima native reserve. He soon found that much of the Ndola rural district was very wild. Within his first week of policing the area, he encountered a pride of seven lions, causing chaos at the Fisenge service station, an elephant creating havoc at the Presenti tomato farm and a leopard that was killing people's dogs on the Kafue small-holdings. He also encountered various herds of game animals, without even leaving the main roads.

Tom's team was also responsible for rail patrol duties, including the north-south main line of rail.

They arrived at the Ndola rail station one Friday, late in the afternoon, when the sky overhead was ablaze with the myriad hues of an African sunset.

Away in the distance, lightning flashed and thunder rumbled as rank upon rank of black storm clouds massed to fill the skies. The frantic bustle around the Ndola station was typical of the end of a long school holiday.

Cars were arriving from towns all over the Copperbelt filled with excited children returning to their boarding schools in Southern Rhodesia or South Africa. There were traffic jams as drivers tried desperately to find a space in the parking area close to the station entrance before the rains came.

Sally Parker, looking around anxiously for a parking, said to her husband, "Charlie, I think someone is about to pull out up ahead there."

"You're right, Mum," her daughter Midge said eagerly. "Come on, Dad, get closer and indicate before someone else grabs it."

Elder sister, Julie, an attractive, blue-eyed blonde, was sitting back and taking in the scene, apparently indifferent to the traffic.

She was far too laid back to betray excitement about something as basic as catching a train, despite the fact that she was the one who would be travelling. However when Midge said, "Look over there, isn't that Peter Sinclair?" Julie suddenly perked up and turned to see where Midge was pointing. A maroon Rolls-Bentley had just driven up and parked in the no-parking area immediately in front of the station steps.

The chauffeur, resplendent in a maroon and gold uniform got out to open the doors for the Sinclairs. He took two suitcases from the boot, gave them to a porter, then pulled away to find a parking spot for the car.

"Oh, Mum, please may I go over and greet Peter?" Julie asked.

"Definitely not," said Sally. "If he wishes to speak to you, he can come over here, Julie. I want you to promise me that you will never become the type of girl who runs after boys."

As general manager of the Nkana mine, Aubrey Sinclair had attained the Copperbelt equivalent of royalty. Julie's father Charlie Parker, on the other hand, as a newly appointed mine captain, had barely placed his foot on the first rung of that ladder.

"Well, a very good evening to you, Mr and Mrs Parker." The mutinous look on Julie's face vanished as quickly as it had appeared. Smiling at them through the window was the handsome face of Jan van Schalkwyk, the star flank-forward of the Roan rugby team.

Julie quickly wound down the window to ask, "What could possibly be important enough to bring you here, Jan?"

"We're here to put my youngest sister Estelle on the train. She's starting boarding school in Salisbury and I have to tell you she's really scared and shy. You must be quite used to this by now, Julie? I wonder would you be prepared to have a chat with her once the train gets going and you've settled-in?"

"For sure, Jan, why don't you bring her over and introduce us right now? It's a long journey and I'm sure it will be good for her to know that she has someone to talk to."

"That's such a nice thought," said Sally, her motherly instincts aroused.

"We've arrived here much too early, Charlie, so there's plenty of time."

Jan didn't waste any time, immediately bringing his sister over to the Parkers' car. She was an attractive blonde and tall for her age. The girls were quickly at ease with one another and they seemed to have plenty to talk about.

Jan said, "I don't know if you have heard about it, Mr Parker, but the action group of the Northern Rhodesian African National Congress have been making threats of sabotage. The police are particularly aware of the vulnerability of our rail links. They have reacted by organising special teams tasked to carry out regular checks along the lines of rail looking for sabotage or any other form of obstruction or damage. The management of Rhodesian Railways have also taken action."

"They have imported specially built motorised inspection cars to facilitate checking the track ahead of the main-line trains. They are generally known as rail-trolleys. My brother Frikkie is to drive the first of these trolleys that is to run ahead of tonight's train. If you don't mind, I thought the girls might enjoy coming with me to meet my brother. They may also want to see the trolley and the police unit that will be responsible for ensuring their safety."

Charlie checked his watch and said, "Yes, we still have a bit of time in hand so I think that's an excellent idea, Jan."

Midge ran on ahead and found the trolley standing, right at the end of the platform. She was surprised to see how small and flimsy it looked compared with the powerful black steam engine that towered over it.

The trolley driver, who was standing in the doorway of the trolley, jumped down quickly when he saw Jan. The brothers gripped each other in a bear-hug. "So, Boet, I've brought our little sister Stelle to see you, she'll be riding in the train behind you tonight. These other young ladies are Julie and Midge Parker; they are also from the Roan."

Midge blushed, giggled and looked away, unaccustomed to being introduced as if she was a grown-up lady. She noticed that a small detachment of uniformed police, comprising an inspector, a sergeant and two constables, had just marched up and come to a halt facing the trolley.

Julie turned to see what was toward. She paid scant attention to the unit as a whole, but she immediately focussed on the inspector. He was in his early twenties, a strongly built young man some six feet in height with dark brown hair and green eyes. A flash of lightning caught the silver of the fish eagle emblem on his cap and the silver bars on his shoulders.

A highly polished black Sam Brown belt and a small strip of colourful active service ribbons on his chest provided some contrast to the sun-bleached beige of his smartly-pressed uniform.

"Well, ladies, it seems that all sorts of things are happening and your carriage should soon be underway, Julie. In fact, it's time for me to return you to your parents. It's been great seeing you, Boet, go well," said Jan, as he led the girls away.

The inspector ordered the sergeant to stand his men at ease. Then he went over to introduce himself to the driver. "Good evening, it's Frikkie van Schalkvyk, isn't it? I'm Inspector Tom Savage. We are to be the duty rail patrol unit responsible for escorting you on the down run to Lusaka tonight."

Frikkie was a tall man, dressed in faded khaki and wearing veldskoon. He was probably in his mid-thirties, very skinny and freckled with a mop of ginger hair and protuberant ears.

Tom said, "I heard Jan van Schalkwyk introduce you as his brother. I don't mean to be impolite but it does seem strange that I don't see any family resemblance?"

"As you say, Inspector Savage, Jan and I are very different because although we had the same father we had different mothers. My mother was very frail and she died when she gave birth to me. My father remarried and Jan is a son that he had with his second wife."

Frikkie; who was a gun enthusiast, had immediately noted the range of weapons being carried by the policemen. The inspector's holstered side-arm was probably a regulation 0.38 special revolver, the sergeant carried a slung 9mm Sten sub-machine gun, the constables were carrying Lee Enfield 303 rifles at the long-port and they wore ammunition pouches. *Well, they are certainly not short of firepower,* he thought. The NRP must be taking the threats made by the NRANC very seriously.

"Will you please get your men aboard the trolley now, inspector, it's time we got underway. My instructions are to ensure that we maintain a relatively constant distance ahead of the train and that will be equivalent to 15 minutes of travelling time at our average speed."

"That's fine, Frikkie, for my part, our job here is simply to check that the track is clear, deal with any untoward security situations that may arise and of course try to avoid getting under your feet."

Savage turned to his sergeant, "Sgt Zulu, embark the men and have them seated on the bench at the rear of the trolley." He climbed aboard then turned to the driver saying, "As you say, Frikkie, it's time we got a move on.

I must say the sooner we can switch off these inside lights the better. They make me feel like an exhibit in a fish tank."

As the trolley pulled away from the platform, Tom took the central swivel seat next to the driver. The inspection car was functional but very basically equipped. However, for Tom and his team, this seemed like a very luxurious way to check the track. He thought of the bicycle patrols they had recently been carrying out along the secondary line of rail between Luanshya and Ndola.

His team had used bicycles to patrol the lines of rail, setting out in the small hours when it was very dark. It was necessary for them to keep their torches and their eyes fixed on the line of rail.

This meant that the riders could not see what lay ahead of them on the narrow path that ran parallel to the track.

Their uniforms and limbs were constantly being ripped to shreds by the overhanging thorn bushes.

There were occasions when more significant injuries were caused especially when someone fell into the one of the many dongas that cut across the track.

There were also interesting variations in these rail patrol accidents. In one instance, a constable rode over and seriously discomposed a large puff-adder. Fortunately, when he fell, he rolled down the bank away from the angry snake.

When selecting teams for rail patrol duty, it came as no surprise that quite a number of officers were suddenly prepared to admit that they had never quite mastered the knack of riding a bicycle!

The trolley quickly gained speed and soon it was virtually running on autopilot, so Frikkie was able to relax. He turned to inquire of Tom, “I don’t recognise those medal ribbons, are they army or police?”

“They are neither, Frikkie; in fact, they are Royal Navy medals.”

“You’re a long way from the sea, inspector, and that makes me wonder how it is possible that you have been awarded naval medals?”

“Please call me Tom, Frikkie. You see I am originally from the UK where on turning eighteen, young men are called up for two years of compulsory national service. I volunteered to serve with the Royal Marines and I was awarded these medals for actions I took part in with 45 Royal Marines Commando in Cyprus and Suez.”

“I must say I envy you, Tom. You have been very lucky to see something of the world, as for myself I’ve never been anywhere outside Northern Rhodesia.”

They were now clear of the outskirts of Ndola. Tom reasoned that this section of the line, being most readily accessible for any activists hiding out in the townships, would be exposed to the greatest risk of sabotage.

Anyone engaged in tampering with the rails would be effectively screened from observation by the dense, encroaching undergrowth.

As the bush closed in on the little rail car, Tom’s eyes and mind were totally focussed on the burnished steel rails, the rail-bed and the bush framed by the wide inspection windows.

Overhead sheets and jagged forks of lightening lit up the sky causing the wall-mounted radio on his right to crackle and squawk.

Then Frikkie’s voice broke in on his thoughts. “I thought I recognised you, Tom, and it’s been bothering me, but I’ve placed you now. I went to watch my boet play in the game against Diggers couple of weeks ago. Weren't you playing at outside-half for the Roan in that game?"

"Yes, indeed and well spotted, Frikkie. I can tell you Diggers play a hard no-nonsense game. I was very glad to have your boet on the flank running interference for me."

Turning to address his sergeant, who was seated with the two constables on a bench to the rear of the vehicle, Tom said, "Sgt Zulu, you can send Constable Kafwembe up front.

He will share lookout duty with me. You and Constable Mooba can stand down for the moment but you must be ready to take over from Kafwembe and me once we reach Kapiri Mposhi."

"Very good, Sah!" Having instructed one of the constables to move to the front of the vehicle, the sergeant pulled his greatcoat about him and settled down to sleep.

Frikkie told Tom, "I can't help thinking that we are probably being watched by 'terrs' right now. They may be planning to ambush the main-line train but what's to prevent them from using our little trolley for target practice."

"I don't think you need to worry about an ambush, Frikkie, it's much more likely that they will attempt to bring about another derailment."

Frikkie went rigid, "What's that you're saying, man, another derailment?"

"I'm sorry, it seems that I have shocked you, Frikkie, I thought that working for the railways you would be in the know. The fact is that a cattle train was derailed in Southern Province a couple of days ago killing a lot of valuable livestock. The NRANC Action Group has claimed responsibility. The whole thing has been kept very low key to prevent them getting too much mileage out of it through the media."

"However, we are concerned that next time they will attempt something so big that it can't be brushed under the carpet."

"Can you imagine the outcry if the 'terrs' were to succeed in derailing the main-line passenger train that is travelling behind us tonight.

Especially since the passengers include hundreds of children returning to school. We have a grave responsibility to ensure that all the people travelling on this train arrive safely in Lusaka."

"I noticed that you called your sergeant Zulu, Tom. Does that mean he is from South Africa then?" Frikkie asked.

"No, Frikkie, that is just his family name, he's not a Zulu by tribe. In fact, he's N'goni from the Lundazi District of Eastern Province. It's true that the N'goni did migrate from South Africa but that was well over a hundred years ago. Their Paramount Chief Zwangendaba led his people north in order to get away from the expansionist aggression of the Zulus. As with all the other Nguni people, if you go back far enough, they all originally migrated from West Africa."

"It sounds as if you have kept yourself busy studying the locals, Tom?"

"It's an important part of my job as rural patrol officer for the Ndola district, Frikkie. The Lamba-Lima Native Reserve forms a large part of my area of responsibility and that means I must represent the queen and sit with Chief Nkana when he holds court."

As he was talking, Tom used a hand control, housed in a panel in the roof above him, to pan a spotlight on the dense bush to either side of the track.

From time to time, the roving light caught startled red or malevolent green eyes crouched in the underbrush, or high in the overhanging canopy.

A stately kudu bull moved cautiously out of cover, the light picking out broken bars of white on his warm beige flanks.

He hesitated for a moment, and then launched himself in a magnificent arc, head up and huge corkscrew horns laid back across his shoulders, clearing the rail-bed in a single bound.

Tom had been holding his breath as he watched entranced. “What a superb animal,” he breathed.

“Let me tell you something, it would be even better if I had it to make some biltong from,” said Frikkie.

“I take it that you like to hunt then, as well as making biltong?” Tom asked.

“Ya, man, whenever I can, but unfortunately I’ve only got a little 0.22 Hornet. It’s the rifle that my oupa gave me when I was a kid. Its fine for killing small game like duiker and steenbok but it’s on the light side for impala, puku or bushbuck.

However, I’m trying to save enough money to buy a real hunting rifle. I want to get a Mauser 7x57. When I get a gun like that I will be able to go after much bigger game like kudu, roan or sable.”

Although Tom wished Frikkie van Schalkvyk well, he found himself hoping that the man would find an alternate method of putting food on the table. It would be sad indeed if

Frikkie were to become completely involved in converting such superb animals into sticks of dried meat.

At that point, a very tall, thin constable came up to the viewing window. Tom said, “Right, Kafwembe, you already know the basic drill, keep your eyes on the move, constantly checking the track and inform me if you suspect there may be anything untoward.

Check the sleepers and the gravel forming the rail-bed; and inform me immediately if you think anything appears suspicious. Should you see anything that may constitute an obstruction on or near the track…”

Kafwembe pointed to a massive grey form that was emerging from the bush a short distance ahead of them. “Excuse me, sir, but would you consider that elephant to be a potential obstruction?”

Frikkie was already slowing the rail car, in order to give right of way to the elephant in question. An elderly matriarch, she was closely followed by several younger cows and two half-grown calves.

Clearly on a mission, the old lady led her little cohort straight across the track where wraithlike the huge grey shapes quickly faded into the dense bush.

Flight 253

“Excuse me, Mr Kaluba.” Justin swivelled his massive head to glare at the speaker, a thin, sandy haired European with a drooping straggly moustache, who had occupied the seat next to him.

“I need to speak to you and I must confess that I contrived to arrange a temporary switch in the seating arrangements in order to create this opportunity. I trust that you don't mind since I can assure you that such a discussion could prove to be mutually beneficial."

A ponderous nod from Kaluba served to indicate that he was prepared to listen.

"Please allow me to introduce myself, my name is James Fitzjohn and I am the political correspondent for the *Liberal Times*."

"I don't know if you are a regular reader of the Liberal, Mr Kaluba? If not, then let me assure you that Northern Rhodesian politics have featured very prominently in my column of late."

"I was privileged to attend the talk you recently gave at the London School of Economics and it made me realise the importance of gaining some in-depth first-hand experience of your beautiful country. While I pride myself on having a very good grasp of current European politics, I must confess that this will be my first visit to Africa."

"When I asked myself who would be best suited to guide me through the potential minefield of Central African politics, I inevitably concluded that there could be no one more eminently qualified than yourself. So much for my motivation, now let us give a moment's thought to what could be in this for you."

"My column features prominently in a widely read weekly newspaper. This would provide you with a wonderful opportunity to express your party's viewpoint. With such an exposure, you can be sure that many households throughout Britain will discuss developments relating to the aims and aspirations of the ZANC over their bacon, egg and cup of tea on a Sunday morning. Such an arrangement would also offer direct financial advantages for you since we will pay well for any useful material or insights you choose to give us."

Kaluba's head had begun to droop, even as Fitzjohn was speaking, but it rose very sharply at the mention of payment.

His bulging brown eyes locked with the washed-out, grey-blue orbs of the columnist as he prompted,

"You said that you will pay well?"

"Oh yes," said Fitzjohn, his moustache fluttering with each breath, "yes indeed." His head nodded rapidly in affirmation, "In fact, I would be prepared to ask my editor if he might consider paying you a regular retainer."

Kaluba's brow creased and he appeared to be engrossed in giving the reporter's proposal serious consideration. He checked his watch, and then he left Fitzjohn to stare at the fold of fat that bulged above his collar, as he turned to look out at the flickering forks of lightning dancing among the huge black clouds that were massed over the Dark Continent. If he happened to catch a glimpse of the single speck of light that moved purposefully through the night far below it held no significance for him.

His thoughts were occupied with a small unit of '*Mpepo kwaNkondo*', (Wind of War) the action wing of ZANC that, at that very moment, should be engaged in putting an important phase of his master plan into effect.

"My plan has come together in a truly wonderful way. What could be better at this very moment in time than being air-born, returning from the UK, and in the process of being interviewed by a British reporter? There can be no allegations that I may have had any direct involvement in tonight's disaster. However, should anyone doubt that a threat from 'Mpepo' must be taken very seriously, tomorrow's headlines will prove that we have the capability to be extremely effective."

He turned back to look earnestly into the pale, freckled face of the newsman.

"Yes indeed, Mr Fitzjohn, I do believe that there is business to be done between us and it should certainly prove to be mutually advantageous."

Rail Trolley

Thunder rumbled and as Tom glanced up he caught a brief glimpse of the navigation lights of a south bound plane between the clouds. "I caught sight of a plane for a moment there, Frikkie, no doubt, this storm will be giving them a rough ride."

Tom took a call on the radio, glanced at his watch and told Frikkie.

"That was Inspector de Laney, who's in charge of the unit on the train. He told me that they passed the Munkulungwe siding about five minutes ago. That means we had better hotfoot it, Frikkie, if we are to stay at least fifteen minutes ahead of them."

The metallic clickety-clack of the wheels increased in tempo and the swaying motion of the rail car became more marked as it sped through the watchful night. For a split second, Tom's spotlight held the sharp face, inquisitive nose, bright eyes and pricked ears of a jackal going about its nocturnal business before it disappeared with a flick of its tail.

A huge pale shape that loomed over the track ahead brought a sharp intake of breath from the lookouts followed by sighs of relief when the lights revealed that it was merely a tree thickly covered in white blossoms.

Racing beneath it, the car was filled with its subtle fragrance.

Then suddenly they were out in the open.

The ground fell away sharply to either side of the track and Tom saw that they were about to cross a river on an elevated causeway.

"That's the Kafulafuta Bridge," said Frikkie. "You can be sure that with all the rain we've been getting the river will be high."

"Sir, I can see some people up ahead, they seem to be working on the track!"

"Thank you, Kafwembe," Tom swung the big roof spotlight to capture three figures in the act of throwing down their tools and plunging down the steeply sloping side of the embankment.

The leader was a slender man of medium height, followed by a huge man, who appeared surprisingly athletic for his size, then bringing up the rear and giving the impression of a terrier snapping at their heels there came a diminutive figure that moved with a strange jerky gait.

The running figures were forced to slow dramatically as they encountered the swampy ground at the foot of the embankment.

As the railcar came to a halt, Tom snapped, "Sgt Zulu, take over the spotlight." Picking up a megaphone, he moved to the open doorway. "You down there, police, halt or I will fire. Iwe, lapa pansi, ma polici, Ima!"

The men ignored his command and continued to wade through the heavy black mud of the dambo bottom.

"Kafwembe, pass me your rifle."

Tom repeated the warning twice as he steadied himself in the doorway and worked the bolt of the Lee Enfield 303. "Very well, keep that light steady, Zulu." He aimed slightly ahead of the leader and squeezed off a warning shot.

The man glanced over his shoulder but didn't pause.

He had almost reached the cover of a bed of reeds when Tom took his second shot.

He aimed at the leading figure but kept it low with the intention of disabling him. He thought he had succeeded when he saw the man stumble before diving into the dense reeds closely followed by his ill-assorted companions.

"Sgt Zulu, take Constable Mooba and see if you can pick up the direction taken by those fugitives.

You will need the short-wave handset, torches and your batons. They did not appear to be armed and one of them may be wounded but don't count on it. When you get to that reed-bed, check if you can find any traces of blood. Also look for any signs that may indicate that they form part of a larger group. Stay together and be on your guard, they may copy the inyati (buffalo) by swinging around and waiting in ambush for you.

They could be heading for Kafulafuta, Luanshya or even Ndola. Call me as soon as you think you have picked up the line they are taking. Do you have any questions? No! Then good luck."

Tom moved back to his station and called Nkhwazi Alpha, the call sign for the larger unit on the train that was led by Inspector Mick de Laney.

"Mick, we have encountered a group of hostiles tampering with the track on the Kafulafuta embankment. I'm not sure of their numbers but we definitely spotted three and I believe I may have wounded one. I suggest you halt the train for the moment but take precautions in case this was a ruse to make us stop."

"Thank you for your concern, Bravo, I trust you have not fired on and injured some innocent villager.

I am quite capable of handling things this end. Since I have no doubt that your three so-called 'hostiles' will have disappeared into the bush without trace, may I suggest that you focus your attention on clearing the track? Our priority now must be to make up some time."

Tom replaced the hand-piece and told Kafwembe, "Stay alert and make sure you secure the immediate area around the trolley. There are likely to be more of them. I should think that there's likely to be at least one lookout and possibly one or two armed men positioned to cover the group that were working on the track."

"As for you, Frikkie, you must hold yourself ready to back the hell out of here at a moment's notice. Now I'm going to check the track and see how much damage those 'terrs' have done."

Tom took out his service revolver to check it, and spun the cylinder out of habit, then replaced it in its holster. Picking up the two-way radio, he clipped it to his belt, took a torch then jumped down his boots crunching on the gravel. Moving cautiously, he followed the footpath that ran alongside the track, aware of the distinctive odour of disturbed swamp gases and rotting vegetation that lingered on the air.

A chorus of sounds rose from the wetland below to fill the night around him. The creaks, chirps and tinkling bell like calls of reed frogs and the deep pitched grunts of bullfrogs provided a pleasant contrast to the high-pitched incessant whine of the bloodthirsty cloud of mosquitoes that hovered around him.

Reaching the section where they had seen the terrorists at work, he found that they had succeeded in virtually dismantling a length of rail. They had certainly come well-equipped to sabotage the track. The tools that they had abandoned included a socket and cross bar assembly that would have enabled them to work on loosening the coach-screws, a pair of small socket spanners that fitted the fishplate bolts, a hammer, pinch-bar and rail tongs.

They had removed two pairs of the fish-plates and appeared to have been engaged in working their way along the rail removing the huge coach-screws that secured it to the Zambezi teak sleepers, when they were disturbed.

If their plan had been successful, then the train carrying several hundred passengers would have plunged down the steep embankment and into the deep, hippo and crocodile infested Kafulafuta River.

Tom shone his torch out across the dark water. He immediately picked up a glowing red eye. As he watched, the crocodile turned its huge head to fix the source of the light with a baleful glare.

The light now held both eyes and Tom was able to gauge the span between them.

That's quite some crocodile, he thought, at a guess he must be all of fifteen feet. I wouldn't want to share the water with him on a dark night, or any other time for that matter.

The radio on his belt crackled. It was Sergeant Zulu reporting in.

"I'm receiving you, Zulu, what is the situation?"

"Sir, we found an area of trampled ground and there was blood on the reeds where the man you shot fell down. We are now following their spoor. They are moving slowly. It is apparent that the wounded man is limping and the other two are supporting him.

They appear to be heading due west so I think they are probably heading for either the Kafulafuta or the St Theresa mission."

"Very good, Sgt Zulu, you've done well. Unfortunately, we can't follow through with the pursuit since the safe passage of the train is our first priority. You must break off now and report back to the trolley as soon as possible."

"It's lucky we got here before they did too much damage," Tom told Frikkie when he got back to the trolley.

"They have abandoned their tools and the fish-plates, bolts and coach-screws are all there. If you lend me a hand, we should soon have the track ship-shape and be on our way. I'll just call Inspector de Laney on the train to ensure that they are in the picture."

"Nkhwazi Bravo to Nkhwazi Alpha, we are effecting repairs to the track and we will be in a position to continue the trolley patrol in about fifteen minutes, over."

Kafulafuta

Ngandu eased himself deeper into the shelter of a bamboo thicket. He realised that although he had been hit, it was only a flesh wound. Nevertheless, it hurt like hell where the bullet had scored a groove just below his left buttock. He thought ruefully that it would be a long time before he could sit in comfort but then he reminded himself he had more important things than comfort to consider.

He had glanced back when it was all happening but he had been so completely dazzled by the spotlight that he was unable to see the officer who had fired the shots.

Nevertheless, he was certain that he would remember that voice with its distinctive northern twang.

Why was it that in his briefing there had been no reference to the presence of a detachment of armed police in a mobile railcar travelling ahead of the passenger train? It may be that the committee had intentionally withheld that vital information?

Could it be that they thought him a coward who might baulk if he were to be made fully aware of the risks involved in this exercise? Ngandu forced himself to shut out the pain and picture the members of the committee.

He attempted to visualise which of them may have been capable of conceiving this type of action.

Justin Kaluba immediately came to mind. *It would be typical of the man,* he thought.

Many of the passengers on the train would be children, heading back to boarding schools in the south. He knew Kaluba well enough to be aware that he was a sadist who had always enjoyed persecuting the younger pupils at the school. He would take pleasure from the deaths of any of the children on the train and relish the thought of the suffering that this would inflict on their parents.

Of course, he could not rule out the possibility that a subtler mind was pulling the strings.

It could even have been a political strategist capable of envisioning that the mission may prove to be more beneficial to the cause if it were to fail. Engineering the drowning of a trainload of schoolchildren is hardly likely to create positive feelings towards us in the UK.

On the other hand, if we were to die ourselves and be skilfully portrayed as a group of ardent nationalists prepared to give our lives for the cause, we would become martyrs or instant folk heroes. Either way, it would provoke a feeding frenzy in the media and be manna for those politicians who wish to rouse the masses from their inertia.

Ngandu was under no illusion about his standing with the committee.

He grinned mirthlessly as he recalled their reaction when, on attending his first action group meeting, he had informed them that he believed they would be more aptly named the NRANC Inaction Group. Many there resented his level of education and the experience and sophistication he had gained while working as a clerk for a legal firm in Chinsali.

Ngandu carefully shifted his position trying to avoid aggravating the pain of his wound. He tried to put it out of mind by recalling the events that had brought him to this place.

It would be a long time before he could sit in comfort but he had more important things than comfort to consider.

Although he had very little involvement with the planning, he realised that he would be the one who would have to carry the blame for the debacle at Kafulafuta.

Why had there been no reference to the fact that a detachment of armed police travelled ahead of the passenger train when he was briefed? Was it because the committee judged him to be a coward who might baulk if he were to be made fully aware of the risks involved?

Ngandu pictured the members of the committee trying to visualise which of them could have conceived this action. When Kaluba recruited him, he had told him, "Simon, the typical masses who flock to join the ZANC chanting 'Kwacha', freedom now and One Man One Vote are merely sheep. If they have any thoughts at all they extend no further than the next piece of meat they will chew on, the brew of beer in their gourd or the woman they want to mount."

"Such men are easily herded in any direction by a clever mind. It is us, the driven, thinking men who are the true freedom fighters and without exception we share a belief that Zambia will only achieve real freedom through violence and bloodshed."

Of course it's quite possible that Kaluba himself is no more than a puppet and above him there is another subtler mind pulling our strings. Why, it could even be KK himself!

As a political strategist, he's quite capable of envisioning that our mission would be most beneficial to the cause if it were to fail.

If only his friends from Kasama could see him now. His clothing ripped to shreds, covered in gore and stinking black mud. A far cry from the Simon Mubanga they thought they knew.

He was totally out of his element in this primeval bush and in desperate need of his childhood companions to guard and guide him.

He suddenly realised that if they failed to come back for him, he may not survive this ordeal and make it back to the civilisation that he craved. For a few blissful seconds, his mind took him back there.

He was the dapper man about town again, in a well-made, grey chalk-stripe three-piece suit, balancing a plate of snacks and a cocktail, while making small talk.

On reflection, he saw that his decision to leave Kasama had been immature and very impetuous. If only he had been more patient, he could have applied himself to study and may eventually have been able to leave as a qualified lawyer.

What was that!

In a heartbeat, he was back in the present, taut and focussed, straining to shut out the incessant sawing of the crickets and a myriad other irrelevant sounds in the darkness around him.

There it was again, the swish of a disturbed branch swinging back into place then he jumped as a dry twig snapped underfoot. His heart was pounding, sweat trickled down his face and his mouth went dry.

There was a very large animal moving through the bush close by.

"Little croc?" Simon recognised the voice and sighed with relief. He took a deep breath and forced himself to sound confident as he called. "I'm over here, mighty elephant; I seem to be stuck in this clump of bamboo. Just give me a hand to get on my feet then you can tell me how you managed to lose the police."

Petros told him, "Jackal and I were ready to lead them a merry dance but they suddenly left our trail, and headed back to the railway line. Doesn't that seem very strange? They must have known that one of us wounded and they had a good chance of catching us."

"We were lucky this time, Petros, the pursuers must have been recalled because the train had a schedule to meet.

However I'm sure they will try to pick up our trail again and it's essential that we be as far from here as possible by first light. Where is the Jackal now?"

"I knew that with your wound, there was no way we could make it to the planned pick-up site in time so I've sent Jackal on ahead to the mission to rouse John, the teacher. They will bring bandages, antiseptic and a pair of trousers for you. They will also bring the mission vanette. We must meet them at the same pick-up site that we used when we came here. I know that it won't be easy going but I'll carry you if necessary."

"Hau! Now I truly believe in the wisdom of elephants.

You have come up with a good plan, Petros. We must move quickly to meet the mission vehicle and get well away from this rural area by morning. We will be easy to recognise as strangers amongst these Lamba peasants. John must take us to the Mikomfwa Township, where we can simply disappear among the masses."

An eerie sound suddenly broke the pregnant silence that had followed the electrical storm.

Starting at a very low pitch, it gradually slid up the scale until it reached a high belling note then it cut off sharply.

"What was that? Surely, they couldn't be using hounds to track us, Petros?" Simon asked anxiously.

Njobvu laughed. "You have been away from the reality of Africa for too long, my friend. That is nothing to worry about, although that hyena does sound rather excited. I'd say that he's probably caught scent of your blood."

"Oh!" said Ngandu a little uncertainly, easing closer to the bulky Njobvu. "I suppose that's okay then."

"Now listen carefully, Petros, John seemed to be very nervous about using the mission's transport to bring us here.

He is probably afraid that he will be disciplined for misuse of the vanette. We must make him even more afraid of what will happen if he doesn't take us to Mikomfwa tonight."

"You must compliment him on his very beautiful young wife. I will say isn't it true that she is pregnant. You can express concern that young girls carrying their first child are so vulnerable. Then I will mention the abundance of young men eager to prove their manhood in the service of the ZANC."

"John may not be brilliant but he is certainly bright enough to realise what will happen to his wife if he doesn't follow my instructions to the letter. Now, as you can see, I have already torn a strip from my shirt to bind up the wound. So if you would be kind enough to cut me a stick to walk with, we can be on our way." With Petros giving Ngandu assistance, they reached the pick-up site where they met up with the mission vehicle.

Mikomfwa

John obeying Jackal's directions drove them into Mikomfwa. "You can pull in here, John, this is the hut," Jackal told him. He jumped out and went to knock on the door. "You can open up, Sally, it is me, Jackal." Petros carried Simon into the hut and laid him on the bed.

"Sally, this is Simon and our huge friend here is Petros."

"But your friend is hurt, what has happened to him?" She asked.

"It is a bullet wound," Jackal told her.

"Very well then, I must talk to my neighbour next door. She is one of us and a nurse at the clinic. I will ask her to bring some antiseptic, a fresh wound dressing and bandages so that she can clean up and dress his wound."

"That's excellent, Sally. May we leave Simon with you for the moment because Petros and I must go to the market to find a change of clothes? It may take some time since I don't have to tell you that it won't be easy to find something to fit Petros." The rain came just as they reached the market so they went into a shebeen and shared a tub of Chibuku beer.

They waited for a while after finishing the beer hoping the rain would ease but it had obviously set in.

They ran from stall to stall through the rain and eventually succeeded in finding a pair of triple x black trousers and an outsize white shirt.

When they got back to the hut, they found that Simon was asleep with a new dressing on his wound. They took off their wet clothing to hang over a chair next to the smoky three legged brazier. Then they put on their new clothes from the plastic bag that they had used to keep them dry. Jackal told Petros that they needed to find somewhere else to stay.

Petros asked, "Why would we want to do that when this place is good?"

Jackal said, "Did you notice the man sitting in the bus station shelter across the road?"

"Yes, I did see him but he is just waiting for a bus."

"I don't think so, Petros. I think he was one of the Nkhwazi that followed our track when we led them by the nose at Kafulafuta. I doubled back to watch them tracking us and I am sure that I recognise him."

Luanshya Central

Tom Savage was sitting in the Luanshya Police Mess, a cold cup of tea at his elbow writing up a rail patrol report when Inspector Mick de Laney burst in.

"Ah, there you are, Savage! You should be glad that I didn't give you a dressing down in front of the Lusaka crowd but I do hope you realise that you're in very hot water.

Not only did you manage to make a mountain out of a molehill last night but you caused a major delay on the down run!"

"I quite understand that you had to line up the rail again and replace a couple of fish-plates but that is hardly a Herculean task. I can assure you that if I had been there I would have had the train on its way in five minutes. As it was, your performance kept us standing there for almost half an hour."

"It's clear to me that all you were dealing with was a couple of villagers trying to help themselves to the metal fish-plates so they could be fashioned into tools. However such an obvious explanation seems to have been insufficiently dramatic for you."

"It's time you realised that we are dealing with simple people here.

They are nothing like the sophisticated EOKA terrorists that you would have us believe you encountered in Cyprus. As if causing such a delay wasn't bad enough, there was worse to come. When I questioned Sgt Zulu just now, he admitted that the villagers were running away when you took it on yourself to fire on them. He said he found blood on the reeds in the dambo and thought you wounded one of them. There will be hell to pay over that, mark my words."

"The officer commanding is sure to be hauled over the coals when word of the incident gets to the ears of the district commissioner. As for you, I promise you'll find yourself facing a court of inquiry."

"I've noticed that you've begun to consider yourself something of a fundi on the native reserve since you took charge of the rural patrols," De Laney snarled. "But we'll see about that after the meeting I have set up with Superintendent Hawkins. You can be sure that he'll have plenty to say when I've given him the facts about the incident you were involved in last night."

Tom willed himself to stay calm. "You should go ahead and make your report, Mick, but when you do remember I'm the one who was on the spot and therefore in touch with what was happening."

"Seeing the reactions of those men when they were caught moving the rail, I had no doubt that they were saboteurs. I believe my conclusion was clearly justified considering the circumstances.

Firstly, there is the evidence of the strategic location especially since there are no villages within miles of that bridge.

The reason for this being that every rainy season the Kafulafuta floodplain is totally inundated."

"Secondly, villagers are very superstitious and are always to be found close to their fire or in their huts after dark. They certainly wouldn't go walkabout at night in a storm. Thirdly, they would never choose to steal from such an exposed situation."

“If the villagers wanted to steal metal, they would choose a place that was not too far from home and where there was thick bush close to the track for cover.”

“I could go on but I think I have proved my point. You see if you are right about them going to so much trouble for a couple of fish-plates then why was it that they had left the loose fish-plates lying on the gravel.

We caught them in the process of trying to move the rail. I can promise you there was no way they intended to steal that rail.

Their plan was to move it out of alignment in order to derail the train. I know something about it because I did some vacation working with a track-laying crew when I was at varsity. Tell me, Mick, do you have any concept of the massive weight and unwieldiness of a full length of main-line rail. It weighs eighty pounds to the yard! Can you imagine the man-power and logistics that would be required to carry such a massive burden across the floodplain?

Finally and most telling of all, we found a full set of track-layer’s tools that these people had abandoned when they fled the scene.”

“In any case, it’s your call, Mick, by all means present your version of the facts to the OC, but I would suggest that you take the opportunity to read through my report before you get too carried away?”

Speechless, Mick de Laney turned on his heel and stormed out of the mess.

“So, Blue, what was all that about?” Inspector Jim Auld had strolled into the mess in time to overhear the tail end of de Laney’s tirade. He turned to the orderly, “Hi there, Musa, can we have two coffees over here?” He sat down and gave

Tom the once-over. "On second thoughts, maybe you'd like something a bit stronger. You're off duty, the sun's going down and you look as if you could use a drink. It'll be my shout and you can have whatever you fancy. That should perk you up a bit you miserable bloody Taff. "

'Jock' Auld was probably Tom's closest friend.

They had been called up in the same draft and completed two years of national service together in 45 Royal Marines Commando.

The strict discipline of the boot camp at Lympstone followed by the rigours of the Commando Training School at Bickleigh had forged a lasting bond. Together they had fought terrorists in Cyprus, Nasser's forces in Suez and even enjoyed a major punch-up with the US Marines of the sixth fleet in Malta.

Finally, when their time was up, they had rebelled at the thought of going back to a boring desk job in the UK. One of their group, Bill Sharp had suggested that they apply to Crown Agents for the Colonies for posts with the Colonial Police.

Tom still felt incredulous when he recalled the day he had first walked into the Luanshya charge office to find Bill Sharp seated behind the desk writing up the occurrence book. Bill had completed his entry then looked up, cool as a cucumber and drawled, "Bit off-course aren't you, 'blue,' as I recall our plan was to meet up in Hong Kong?"

"Hello there, is there anybody at home? It must be pretty serious for you to allow your mind to go walkabout for so long, especially when I've just offered to buy you a whisky."

"Sorry, Jock, and thanks for the offer but I think I will pass. The only thing that might perk me up right now will be a few hours in the sack. My section was on rail patrol duty to

Lusaka last night and we came back on the up train arriving in the small hours so I haven't managed to catch a wink of sleep."

"You see, we came across some characters busy dismantling the rails at the Kafulafuta Bridge. They took off and when they kept running despite my challenges I fired a warning shot. They kept going I took a disabling shot that nicked their leader. Mick de Laney's section was on the train and he has got his knickers in a knot about my actions."

"He believes that I overreacted and they were only some thieving villagers. He has gone off to see the OC intending to convince him that I'm a trigger happy cowboy."

"Relax, Tom; you don't really know de Laney. As rural patrol officer, you've spent so much time away from the station 'bundu bashing'. I grant you he's a bit of an 'old woman' but once you can see past that, he's not so bad."

"Worst case is he'll suggest to the OC, in a thousand words, that you need to be disciplined. There's no way he'll suggest that you get the bullet."

The phone rang and Jim Auld picked up, He listened for a moment then said, "Yes sir, he's on his way." Replacing the phone, he told Tom, "The OC wants you to report to his office immediately Taff. It's better this way; at least you'll know where you stand when you finally hit the sack. Just get in there, state your case, and the very best of British."

Superintendent Geoffrey Hawkins looked up as Tom came to a halt at the open doorway of his office. "Come in, Savage." Tom marched forward, came to attention in front of the desk and snapped off a salute.

"At ease, Savage, you can leave that report in my in tray for the moment, just take a seat.

I want you to talk me through the incident you were involved in on rail patrol last night."

"Well, sir, as you no doubt know, my team have been carrying out bicycle patrols checking the secondary railway line to Ndola. That was an extremely arduous task so it was a very welcome surprise to find that we would be travelling in a mechanised rail trolley to precede the main-line train."

"The train that would follow us was packed with school children who were returning to schools down south after the holidays. Things went smoothly until we reached the Kafulafuta rail-bridge where we saw that there were men engaged in interfering with the track. As we approached, they threw down their tools and ran down the embankment."

"I stood in the doorway of the trolley and shouted a command ordering them to stop but they ignored me. I warned them to halt or I would fire. I was holding a rifle that I had taken from one of the constables. The terrorists had not gone too far because of the heavy going they had encountered when moving through the mud of the dambo bottom. When they failed to stop I fired a warning shot."

"Then as they were about to plunge into a thick bed of reeds, I fired a second shot keeping it low with the intention of wounding their leader. He fell and I felt sure that my shot had hit him in the leg. Then I radioed Inspector de Laney, who was aboard the train, to warn him that the trolley had been delayed. I told him that I would inform him as soon as we were on the move again."

"I instructed Sgt Zulu to take Constable Mooba and track the insurgents but to return quickly as soon as he had established the direction they were taking. Then I went to examine the condition of the rail they had been working on."

"They had removed enough coach-screws and fish-plates to enable them to move the heavy rail out of line. Their intention was obviously to derail the train so that it would plunge into the river. They had abandoned a complete set of track layers tools and a heavy pinch-bar that they must have used to lever the track out of line."

"I took Constables Kafwembe and Mutuna to help me lever the length of rail back into line then we re-installed the coach-screws and fish-plates. When Sgt Zulu returned, he informed me that my shot must have hit its target because he had found blood on the reeds.

"From their tracks, it was obvious that the terrorists were now moving slowly and obliged to support their wounded leader. Zulu was eager to follow up in hot pursuit feeling sure that it would be possible to catch them. I congratulated Zulu on a job well done but explained that our first priority must be to get the train underway.

"He appears to have established that the criminals were heading for either the Kafulafuta or the St Theresa mission and I assured him that we would certainly follow that up after we handed over the security of the train to the duty shift in Lusaka."

"Thank you, Savage; I am quite satisfied with your handling of this matter. By the way, that was a good shot but it was only to be expected since I see you were classed as a marksman in the marines."

I would like you to make an early start tomorrow. "Take your team to St Theresa and make thorough enquires to establish if the terrorists were there last night. You should check with the sister at the clinic because it is quite likely that they would have asked her to dress that wound." Arriving at

St Theresa's mission, Tom pulled the Land Rover deep into the shade cast by a huge old Natal Mahogany tree.

"Very well, Sergeant Zulu, I must go and talk to the mother superior or the senior cleric or whoever is presently in charge here to obtain their permission to question the sisters and any local staff. I will also ask for the use of an office where we can take statements if necessary."

"Meantime, I want you to look around, speak to any of the people you encounter and determine if any of them are aware of strangers visiting the mission recently. Instruct the constables to help you with this but you should take over yourself if they encounter something that is worth following up."

A wide covered veranda helped to keep the temperature within the admin block bearable and Tom felt the contrast the moment he stepped out into the full glare of the sun. He made his way across an open square of baked earth heading for the clinic.

This was a long low building with a red corrugated iron roof its utilitarian lines softened by a stand of eucalypts.

The attendant collection of thatched shade huts made him think of a mother hen with a rather motley flock of chickens. The area was crowded since each patient waiting to be examined and administered to by the sister was accompanied by a retinue of relatives and friends.

Tom was walking past one of the thatched shade huts when he heard someone playing a kalinka.

He looked over the low wall and saw that there was an attentive audience surrounding the musician who was sitting on the floor with his back against the centre pole.

The player chanted snippets of local news while his fingers skilfully flicked the wires of the simple hand piano.

The crowd was animated, laughing and exclaiming at items of scandal from the neighbouring villages.

However, when he made reference to Chief Nkana, they immediately became silent, lowering their heads and clapping their hands as a mark of respect.

Suddenly, sensing Tom's steady regard, the player lifted his head and turned to say, "I see you bwana, Savage."

"I see you, Shamwali (friend)," said Tom, "what is the nature of the business that you have here?"

"I have been troubled by a jigger bwana and I have come to ask the lady doctor to give me some muti (medicine)."

When Shamwali unwrapped the rag that he had bound around the injured foot, it revealed a deep suppurating cavity.

A universal 'ahhh' of sympathy escaped the crowd as they all leaned forward to examine his wound.

"You must remember for next time that it would have been better if you had waited for the sister to take out that jigger.

You probably used a dirty thorn to dig it out and now you have a bigger problem."

"Aiee! I am but a poor man bwana that carries news from village to village in exchange for a meal and shelter. I was very far from a clinic and I had to try something because the pain of that worm feasting in my flesh was driving me mad."

"I hope the sister has strong medicine to make you well. Don't go away, Shamwali, we must talk when you have finished giving the people their news."

"Inde bwana, I will be waiting here."

Tom ran up the red polished steps to the clinic.

“Mwapoleni mukwai,” (greetings) a young cleaner greeted him with a flashing smile.

A brush under one foot and a rag under the other, he was executing a shuffling dance to the tune of Shamwali’s kalinka as he polished and buffed the stoep.

“Eya mukwai. (greetings to you) Do you know where I may find either the reverend father or the mother superior?”

“I’m sorry, sir, but they are not available. They left early this morning because they had to go to a meeting in Ndola.”

“So who is in charge now?”

“That would be Sister Maria, sir; she is standing in for Sister Faith.”

“I must say you speak English very well for a cleaner!”

“That is because I not just a cleaner, sir. I am a student at the school here. I am on detention and I have been given the job of polishing these floors as my punishment.”

“Very well, keep up the good work then. Where can I find this sister?”

“Just go through that door behind you, sir, she is busy seeing to the patients.”

Tom entered the room and closed the door quickly behind him to keep out flies. A breath of air from the labouring ceiling fan felt good on his sweat beaded face.

He studied a slender figure in crisp hospital whites.

Definitely not Sister Faith, the chunkily built, down to earth Geordie that he had met previously at the clinic.

“Get out! Who gave you permission to come barging in here?” The sister’s lovely face was flushed and her eyes flashed as she looked up from administering an enema to a patient.

Tom turned back to the door saying. "My apologies Sister, however, I would like to speak to you as soon as you are free."

Back on the stoep and feeling somewhat chastened, Tom found collecting his thoughts surprisingly difficult. What an incredible woman, she definitely gets a ten for looks in my book.

I wonder what's happened to Sister Faith.

This one may look like an angel but she seems to have the devil of a temper. With that name, those 'Gina' looks and that temperament I'd hazard a guess that she's Italian.

He found the student still busily dancing and polishing the same spot on the stoep and enquired if he knew the sister's full name.

"She is called Sister Maria Gianelli, sir, and she is to be here while Sister Faith is away on leave."

The door behind Tom swung open. "That's all right, Michael, you can carry on with your work. I will deal with the officer. So, inspector, what worldly crisis has brought you charging in where angels fear to tread?"

"Good morning, Sister, I am Inspector Tom Savage from Luanshya Central. I am the officer responsible for the Ndola rural district and that includes the Lamba-Lima reserve. While I know you must be very busy, I would appreciate it if you could give me a minute of two of your valuable time. Is it possible for us to have a talk somewhere that is not quite so open to the public?"

"Very well, inspector, just follow me and we'll go through to the office."

The 'office' proved to be a closet-sized room furnished with a tiny table, two straight backed chairs and a plank raised on two bricks to act as a bookcase.

It was so small that there was barely space to pull out a chair so Tom decided to stand.

"I am following up on an incident of attempted sabotage of the main line of rail that took place the night before last on the Kafulafuta embankment. I believe that in addition to the mission hospital, you operate a small medical clinic for the benefit of members of the local community?"

"One of the saboteurs was slightly wounded and I believe it possible that he may have come to this mission for treatment. I would like to ask the sister in charge of the clinic if she was asked to dress an injury that may have been a bullet wound yesterday in the early morning hours."

Sister Maria told him that she was in charge and she had not been required to treat a wounded man however the clinic had been broken into during the night and bandages, lint and ointments were stolen.

Tom went back to question Shamwali who told him that he had spent the night in the rest hut.

He had been woken up when three strangers arrived at the clinic in the early hours.

It was dark and they did not notice him but he could see that one of them was extremely large and another, who was very small, was walking as if one leg was much shorter than the other. He knew that they were not locals because they were speaking Chibemba.

They had called their group Mpepo and he heard them talking about hiding in Mikomfwa. Then the big one went to get the driver.

"Did you hear anything else of interest in your travels, Shamwali?"

"Yes indeed, sir, some of the villagers, who have been into town, say that they were told of a Bemba woman called Alice Lenshina. They say that she became very sick and she was in a coma when she went to heaven and had a meeting with Jesus Christ. He told her that she must start a new church called the Lumpa Church. Her church has become very strong and she already has tens of thousands of followers not only here but also in the Congo, Nyasaland and Tanganyika."

At that point, Sgt Zulu came to make his report.

He told Tom that in questioning the staff, he had learned that the driver was in trouble for making unauthorised use of the mission vehicle.

When Tom went to examine the vehicle, a small white Austin vanette, he found the driver busy cleaning it.

He asked him, "Did you see any strangers around the mission last night?"

"No sir, the people were staying indoors because of the rain."

"I see that this vehicle is very muddy, so tell me where did you take it last night?"

"It was raining quite heavily, sir, so I had to drive two of the maids home. As you can see the track I had to take to get to their kia was very muddy."

"Are you quite sure that is all you did? You had better tell me the truth because I assure you that I will check the mileage on the vehicle with Sister Maria?"

"Yes sir, well I must admit that I did also go to see my family and my home is some distance away. I am the fifth child and my parents are getting old. Also I have my young wife staying with them."

"I see, so how long did you stay with them?"

"I think it must have been about an hour, sir."

Lusaka

Kaluba was on edge waiting for a report and when the phone rang He picked up the receiver and snapped, "Kaluba."

"Ngandu here, sir, I am calling from Mikomfwa."

"Don't waste my time with minor details, Ngandu; just tell me about the derailment. Do you have any idea how many people were killed? Is there a report in this morning's paper?"

"I am sorry, sir, but I have to tell you that we were unable to derail the train. There was a police unit…"

"What you are saying is that you have failed miserably," Kaluba cut in, "you, the loudmouthed critic, who told the regional assembly at Chinsali that you would show us how to make things happen. I went to great lengths to ensure that you were provided with the transport, the tools and three good men."

"Yet still you have failed to move one end of a single length of rail the few inches that would be necessary to bring about a derailment. You are pathetic, Ngandu! You are no kind of leader! I want Njobvu to assume temporary command of that group while I organise your replacement."

"Please hear me, sir. I believe it to be essential that our group should do its own scouting and planning before attempting any action of this nature. In this instance, if I had known that the police routinely patrol the track ahead of main-line trains, I would have employed an alternative plan."

Kaluba took deep breaths and forced himself not to react to Ngandu's casual dismissal of his brainchild since he had initiated the action himself.

Unfortunately, he had been so preoccupied with preparations for his visit to London that he had failed to spend time working on the details of its execution.

Any investigation by the committee may very well determine that the plan failed as a result of his ineffective groundwork.

He inquired icily as to the nature of Ngandu's alternative plan.

"Sir, there is a window of opportunity that would give us at least five minutes between the transit of the inspection car and the track being illuminated by the headlights of the oncoming train. While that time is too short to dismantle a rail, I believe it would suffice for us to plant an explosive charge."

Kaluba virtually exploded. "This is incredible! You have accomplished absolutely nothing to justify my faith in you and now you have the nerve to expect me to wave a magic wand and provide you with explosives."

"I'm sorry, sir, please allow me explain how I intend to make this plan work. I found it necessary to split up the group when we reached Luanshya."

"Myself, I am slightly wounded, so I have found a bed in the home of Mary Mulenga one of our ZANC ladies in Mikomfwa Township. Her boyfriend Silas is a night shift boss boy from the mine and he is a blasting licence holder. He was very suspicious when he arrived home early this morning to find me in his house."

"However, I have managed to convince him that I am not trying to steal his girlfriend and I think he might be prepared to help us for a price."

"Ngandu, this is all too little and too late, you don't seem to understand the extent of your failure. Because of your ineptitude, we have missed the opportunity to derail the annual school train. That train is always filled with hundreds of children going back to boarding schools down south after their Christmas holiday. If it had plunged into the river, the effect would have been devastating."

"Not only would the papers have been full of it but also half the ex-patriots on the Copperbelt would have been weeping their eyes out as they packed their bags and headed back to Britain. I have been very patient listening to you spell out your dreams, Ngandu. Now let me explain something very basic to you, it's only results that count."

"You will receive no more funding until I see results from your group. You can consider yourself very lucky that I have decided to give you one more chance and a worthwhile contact. You can ask your hostess Mary Mulenga to arrange that you meet a young man named Picson Chanda."

"The nucleus of his youth group is quite small but given a few hours' notice, Picson can put together a useful crowd. I will speak with him and tell him to expect you to call on him when you are in need of numbers. Take note, the next time I hear from you, it must be in the press. I want to see a crop of headlines reporting extensive damage to government property, civil disturbances, strikes and general unrest on the Copperbelt. Remember that time isn't on your side," Kaluba warned Ngandu, "because I shall be actively engaged in looking for the man to replace you should you fail again."

Heindriks Brewery in Luanshya had created an attractive beer-garden with lawns, benches and tables under thatched shade huts. It was a popular venue especially at the weekend.

Therefore, there was major resentment among the off-duty miners who had brought their families planning to enjoy the peaceful ambiance when they arrived to find the splintered tables and benches sitting amongst the smouldering remains of the thatched huts. There were numerous spray painted signs that stated that this was the handiwork of the ZANC youth movement.

When Sally told Simon of the destruction of the beer-garden, he told her, "This action of the ZANC youth is badly misjudged. It will only serve to make us very unpopular. Please tell Picson that he must come and have a meeting with me."

Luanshya Central

During his return from the mission, Tom called in at the Mikomfwa sub-station. He told the sergeant in charge that he must instruct his constables that they should be on the lookout for a group of three men. One of them being unusually large, a second who was very small and had a strange limping gait and a third who was lightly wounded.

Back at Luanshya Central, Tom went to report to Superintendent Hawkins. He informed him of the results of their enquiries at Kafulafuta. He told him that he had made the sergeant at the Mikomfwa sub-station aware of the attempted sabotage of the train and given him a description of three of the men who were involved.

"Very good, Savage, I believe your rural patrol team must be slightly understaffed for this type of surveillance so I have arranged for two additional constables, Musonda and Mutasa to be transferred to you team. They are both Lamba from the area where you are working and they should fit in well.

They will be able to blend in with the community and communicate with the locals without their surveillance of the hut being too obvious."

"I suggest your next move should be to take Sergeant Zulu and his team and carry out a slow patrol of Mikomfwa focussing on the market, Chaisa Hall and the shops. Their wounded member is probably lying up in a hut but the other two must be feeling quite confident now that they can mingle with the crowds."

"Do not make any attempt to contact the two special branch constables, Lamumba and Nyoka, even if you should see them, since they are there undercover."

Tongalulu Section

The team was making a second circuit of the area when Kafwembe exclaimed, "Look over there!"

Tom caught a glimpse of an oddly assorted couple entering a hut some distance away.

"Well spotted, I think you may be right Kafwembe.' I believe you know Mikomfwa quite well, Mooba, what is the name of this section?"

"I have heard people call it Tongalulu section, sir."

"Thank you, Mooba. Make a note of the location of that hut, Zulu.

It may be that it is being used as a meeting place for Mpepo. Constable Mooba, when we get back to the station, you must immediately change into plain clothes. I will be bringing you back here so you must take this opportunity to have a good look around. Try to find yourself a position that will allow you to watch that hut without being too conspicuous."

"I should be able to observe the hut from the bus shelter I can see on the other side of the road, sir. I'll sit on the bench apparently waiting for transport. It will also afford me some shelter since it looks as if it may rain."

"That is very good, Mooba. When we come back to Mikomfwa, I will drop you at the market, since you must not be seen to arrive in a police vehicle.

Begin by mingling with the crowd before you make your way on foot to the shelter. I noticed a clothing store that we passed a short distance from here, do you happen to know at what time they close?"

"I believe they close at about 6:00pm, sir."

"Very well then, when that shop closes, you must go and wait in their doorway. That is where I will come to collect you and drop off Kafwembe who will relieve you. That hut is to be kept under a 24-hour watch."

When he made his report, Constable Mooba told Tom that he had recognised Justin Kaluba, a notorious ZANC activist. Kaluba had come in the dusk to enter the hut that housed the terrorists.

Mikomfwa

Jackal asked Sally, "I wonder why is it that you do not have an effective youth movement here on the Copperbelt?"

She told him, "Jackal, it is true that the youth group here is relatively small. I believe it has about thirty-five members led by a young man called Picson Chanda. However, if they were to have a charismatic and active leader like Simon Kapwepwe, then I am certain that there would be an abundance of young men flocking to join our movement."

"I think that I should make arrangements for Picson and his lieutenant Jackson Sibanda to come and have a meeting with you."

When Sally went next door to see Mary, Jackal said, "Come on now, Simon Ngandu, you must pull yourself together. It's time you stopped nursing that scratch. You heard what Sally had to say, they need someone like Kapwepwe to stir up the youth here and who could we hope to find who would emulate Kapwepwe better than you?"

Luanshya Central

When Tom got back at Central, he reported the sighting of Kaluba to Superintendent Hawkins who said, "That is very interesting, Savage, so Kaluba has come up from Lusaka! You may not be aware of it but Kaluba is a protégé of Simon Kapwepwe. He is on the fringe for now but it is obvious that he has hopes of making his mark with the top brass of the ZANC."

"We have managed to minimise the coverage that the media has given to their derailment of a train carrying cattle in the southern province that involved a serious loss of valuable livestock."

"However, it may very well be that it was Kaluba who motivated this latest attempt to derail a train, especially since the target this time was a main-line train loaded with school children. If an action of that nature was to be successful it would be far too big a story to be kept under wraps."

"It is Kapwepwe who initiated and heads up Mpepo kwa Nkondo (Wind of War) a militant faction that he has established within the core of the ZANC. Their members use Mpepo as a code word to recognise one another."

"It is possible that the members of Mpepo are using that hut as their meeting place. You must make a plan to keep it under twenty-four hour surveillance.

Your watchers should be positioned so that they are able to observe any coming and going. But you must ensure that the presence of any member of your team in the vicinity is not too conspicuous."

Sergeant Zulu told Tom, "Sir, I believe Sergeant Mbambala has a cousin who lives in Tongalulu section. It may be possible to negotiate with him for the use of his hut as a base for our watchers."

"That is an excellent idea, Zulu; I will ask Sergeant Mbambala if he would be prepared to broach the matter with his cousin."

Mpepo

Sally introduced Picson Chanda and Jackson Sibanda of the youth movement to Ngandu, Jackal and Petros of Mpepo.

Jackal took the floor and told them, "Our leaders have met in Ndola. They are strongly opposed to colonialism and the federation that has been initiated and is controlled by the government in Salisbury. They have ordered that we must begin a campaign of violence initially focussing on the murder of farmers and small holders."

Jackal said, "Petros, you must remember what I told you! It is obvious that the Nkwazi do not have sufficient numbers to keep constantly changing the watchers. I will make a good plan for our move to Muliashi and when I do they will have completely lost track of us I must go out now to find new quarters and a vehicle for us." Jackal was away for quite some time. When he finally did come back, he was driving an old red Combi.

It was rusty and it looked like a wreck but its engine sounded surprisingly healthy.

"Hello Sally, please ask Mary to come over."

"Hello there, Mary, how is our patient coming along?"

"He's much improved, Jackal, that ointment you obtained has been very effective. You must have noticed that we are under close observation here, Mary? Do you think it will be possible for me to organise to move him to another safe house tomorrow?"

"With care and provided the going isn't too rough, that should be fine," Mary told him.

"Good, so tomorrow morning, I would like both of you and a few of your friends to meet in front of this hut and have a noisy argument. Make it loud enough to distract the constable while we get Simon and Petros into the vehicle."

The ruse was successful but then as they were driving past, Maclaren Shaft a police car pulled them over.

Jackal pointed to Simon's bandaged leg and told the policeman that that they were taking their injured friend to the clinic.

The policeman said, "That's all very well but you must turn back because you will not be allowed to use the mine clinic and the government clinic is in town." He also gave Jackal a warning for having an illegible rear number plate.

They headed back until the police car turned into Churchill Avenue. Then they doubled back onto the Muliashi Road.

Jackal asked Simon if it would be necessary for them to slow down when they got onto the gravel road heading out to the Muliashi farming area.

Simon told him not to worry because the graze on his buttock was not troubling him unduly. Petros said, "That's very good news, well done, Simon. I'm glad to hear that you are pulling yourself together."

Their rusty Combi handled the gravel road quite well and it wasn't long before they reached Muliashi. Jackal turned off down a narrow overgrown track that eventually took them to a dilapidated hut. He told them, "We can use this hut as our base when we begin our campaign against the small-holdings and outlying farms. I have paid a couple of villagers to repair the thatch sufficiently enough for it to keep out the rain."

"There is a very old couple, the Bradleys, who have a small holding and store nearby. They are highly respected in the area and their murder will send a message.

Once we have eliminated them, then we can take all the supplies we need for our base from their store."

Luanshya

Superintendent Hawkins called a meeting with Chief Inspector Green, the head constable and his sergeants. He told them of the meeting of ZANC leaders in Ndola. "Special branch have informed me that their plan is to instigate a campaign of violence, initially focussing on isolated farms and small-holdings. It will be difficult for us to provide protection against such actions."

"Ideally, the people from the outlying properties should move into town but this will not always be possible. The frequency of random visits by rural patrol must be increased and non-commissioned officers should be armed."

A special branch officer informed Superintendent Hawkins that Mpepo had called a meeting in Chaisa Hall to discuss their plans for a Night of The Long Knives in Luanshya. He immediately called the mobile unit in Bwana Mkubwa to request reinforcements.

When they received confirmation, Tom drove down the main road to meet up with the mobile unit force.

He led them along back roads to where they could park their vehicles at the rear of the Roan Antelope sub-station. They were joined by an NRP contingent from Luanshya central. When the drumming and the singing came to a peak, the combined force moved out to surround Chaisa Hall and arrest all the members of the action group Mpepo that were present.

Tom was aware of the presence of a second Mpepo group in Muliashi. They were responsible for the murder of the Bradleys. He asked the mobile unit commander to delegate a section of his force to supplement the Nkwazi that would be going to Muliashi to deal with any remaining Mpepo.

Muliashi

Petros and Jackal had broken into the back room of the Bradley's store where they found a good stock of beer and spirits.

It took several trips to carry their booty to their hut where they were joined by a number of youth group members who participated in their celebrations.

Long before the combined force reached the Mpepo hut, they could hear drumming and many voices singing Kwacha songs. They met little resistance from the drunken Mpepo members as they rounded them up and loaded them into the vehicles. However, when Tom checked the prisoners, they were holding he found that Ngandu had escaped their net.

Put under intense pressure, Jackal divulged that Ngandu had told him of a secure hideaway at Kashiba where the Nkwazi would never find him.

Tom remembered Shamwali telling him that the Lamba villagers in the area were fearful of approaching the lake especially at dusk. Some years ago, the little Bushmen, on finding themselves unable to prevent the Lamba Lima tribesmen from taking their attractive little women as slaves, had committed mass suicide by jumping into the deep lake and drowning themselves. The villagers believe that the lake is haunted by the spirits of the WaMbusi people.

The darkly coloured, nocturnal tree dassies are plentiful at Kashiba. They become active at dusk when their eerie screams echo around the sunken lake.

Also at nightfall, numerous ghostly lights appear amongst the trees. They are emitted by phosphorescent fungi.

Tom took Sgt Zulu and Constable Kafwembe—who was excellent at tracking—to Kashiba in order to try and find Ngandu. At first, they were unnerved by the eerie lights until he showed them the fungi that were the light source.

It was dusk and the lighting was poor but Kafwembe still detected signs of damaged vegetation as they followed

Ngandu's passage through the dense growth on the lake's southern rim.

Ngandu was hiding in the thick bush when the tree dassies began to call all around him.

He thought that he was hearing the lost souls of the Mbusi people. He ran in panic and blundered into an ancient hollow tree where he suddenly found himself face to face with a huge grey-black crested snake. The mamba struck, sinking its fangs deep into his neck. Ngandu screamed to Tom for help. When Tom burst out of the bush, Ngandu begged to be taken to the clinic.

Tom told him that no one could help him now.

Death from the bite of a mamba came very quickly.

He should rather make use of the last few moments of his life preparing himself to meet his maker.